Uncertain Death

Sheila Malory has travelled to Birmingham to speak at a literary lunch but even at such a distance from home she cannot avoid her unpleasant neighbour, poet and biographer Adrian Palgrave, who has been asked to speak at the same event. Unfortunately Palgrave is even more smug than usual for he has just had a piece of good news – he has been appointed literary executor of the late Laurence Meredith, well-known author and socialite, which should provide him with a lucrative and prestigious literary scoop.

Once back in her home village of Taviscombe, Sheila is swept up in the organization of the local festival, which sees her spending more time than she would like in the company of Palgrave, who is also on the festival committee. His overbearing manner makes him unpopular with almost everyone, particularly the committee's newest recruit, a nervous young accountant who leaves a meeting on the verge of tears after a savage verbal attack by Palgrave. Who could have guessed, however, that the first event of the Taviscombe Festival was to prove Adrian Palgrave's last?

The Taviscombe community is deeply shocked by news of Adrian Palgrave's murder and because she knows the local networks so well, Sheila Malory is approached by the police to make some subtle enquiries. When another death occurs it appears that Sheila is on the trail of a ruthless double killer. And she must investigate the clandestine affairs of the present before long-buried secrets can be unmasked . . . secrets which have prompted someone to kill and kill again . . .

Uncertain Death

Hazel Holt

MACMILLAN
LONDON

First published 1993 by Macmillan London Limited

a division of Pan Macmillan Publishers Limited
Cavaye Place London SW10 9PG
and Basingstoke

Associated companies throughout the world

ISBN 0–333–58521–6

9 8 7 6 5 4 3 2 1

A CIP catalogue record for this book is available from
the British Library

Phototypeset by Intype, London
Printed by Mackays of Chatham Plc, Chatham, Kent

FOR JAN
with love

Chapter One

Because I managed to get myself lost in the Harborne one-way system, it was early evening when I got to the hotel. The M5 had been full of indecisive caravans, thrusting young men in Sierras and the Daf Racing Lorry Team, so I felt pretty exhausted. I threw my bag and coat on to the bed and switched on the television and the electric kettle. I was pleased to see that the 'tea-making facilities' included a couple of chocolate wafer biscuits and that there was conditioner as well as shampoo in the bathroom. Not that I planned to wash my hair (I was only going to be staying one night) but it gave me a feeling of agreeable luxury. I love staying in hotels, just for a short time – after a few days I get restless and want my own things around me and I miss the animals – but for a little while I greatly enjoy this enclosed, private world, where everything one might want is conveniently to hand.

I had travelled to Birmingham from my home in the West Country to speak at a Literary Lunch, organized by a large bookstore. This isn't something that happens to me very often – the books I write are usually considered too academic – but the latest one was a study of the writer Ada Leverson and the connection with Oscar Wilde made it 'popular' enough for the organizers of the Lunch to feel that people (as opposed to academics) might want to listen to me for fifteen minutes or so. I hate speaking in public – the sound of my voice, on the rare occasions when I've heard it on a tape-recorder, makes me shrivel up with embarrassment – but in a weak moment I said yes and I'd been fervently regretting it ever since.

There were to be three speakers and I'd asked to be the first so that I wouldn't have to sit through the others, getting more and more nervous. Especially since one of the other speakers was Adrian Palgrave, whom I knew and disliked. He is, in effect, a neighbour, living in a converted schoolhouse in a village just outside Taviscombe. I suppose you might describe him as a well-known poet and broadcaster – 'well known for being well-known', as my son Michael says – and he is, in his own opinion at least, a prominent literary figure. Perhaps I am being just a little sour because he has made it very clear that he thinks of me as a mere amateur. He is always affable, but with a patronizing air that I find very irritating indeed. I sincerely hoped he wouldn't be staying in the hotel, though since the Lunch was to be held there on the following day, I very much feared he might. It was with this thought in mind that I went down to the dining room early, feeling that he would be more likely to dine fashionably late. I ate my food quickly with my head bent low over my book and then retreated to the safety of my room. After I had read through my speech one more time and wondered if anyone would find it remotely interesting, I had an enjoyable evening watching a thriller on television and doing my nails.

The high-spot of any stay in a hotel for me is the Full English Breakfast. At home I rarely have more than a slice of toast and a cup of tea, but when I'm away I always go the whole hog. This particular morning my plate was deliciously full of bacon, egg, tomatoes, mushrooms, black pudding, and fried bread and I sat and contemplated it with satisfaction. I had just unfolded my *Daily Telegraph* and was giving myself over wholly to pleasure when I was aware of a figure standing beside me. It was Adrian Palgrave.

'Ah, Sheila. May I join you?' he asked and without waiting for my reply he sat down.

He went droning on about how tiresome it was to have to come all this way to speak at this tedious luncheon but

8

one did have a duty to one's publisher. Needless to say, his breakfast consisted of half a grapefruit and a black coffee. Fortunately he didn't seem to require any actual verbal response so I was able to get on with my food, but the treat was ruined and I was thoroughly put out.

'I must say I was surprised that they asked Alicia Nash to be the other speaker. I mean, she is a highly competent actress – she was in one of my radio plays – but hardly a *literary* figure.'

'She has just written a book,' I replied. The fried bread was very crisp and a piece shot off my plate when I cut into it. Adrian looked at my still substantial plateful with some distaste and said: 'Memoirs. Anecdotes, really.'

'I haven't read it,' I said, 'but they say it's very amusing.'

Adrian scrutinized my plate more carefully.

'Should you be eating all that fried stuff?' he asked. 'I suppose you know it's crammed with cholesterol and statistics have shown that middle-aged women are just as liable to heart-attacks as middle-aged men.'

I did not need Adrian Palgrave to remind me that I am a widow in my mid-fifties. I bit into a piece of black pudding defiantly.

'At my advanced age,' I said, 'this is the only way left to live dangerously.'

He gave me a brief humourless smile and went on.

'I hope the book-signing afterwards doesn't go on too long. I've got to get to the Pebble Mill studios for an interview this afternoon.'

'I don't imagine *my* book signing will take any time at all,' I said. 'I expect I shall just stand there with a pile in front of me feeling embarrassed. What a pity I can't sign *your* books for you.'

This frivolous remark on such a serious subject was not considered worthy of a smile of any kind and he continued.

'I went to the new Concert Hall yesterday evening. The acoustics are superb. They were doing *Gerontius*. I was

9

following with a score, of course, and every note was like crystal! Quite magnificent. I rather expected to see you there – such an opportunity!'

I thought guiltily of the thriller on television and said quickly: 'Oh, I arrived rather late . . .'

He pushed aside his half-eaten grapefruit and leaned across the table. 'I was thinking, as I sat there, that we really must make a special effort with the music for this year's festival. We need something really unusual – a new piece specially commissioned or some international musician.'

'I don't really imagine that we could attract anyone of international standing to the Taviscombe festival,' I protested.

Adrian regarded me earnestly.

'I think you underestimate the influence that I and some of our other more important residents may have, Sheila,' he said reprovingly. Certainly our particularly picturesque corner of the West Country has attracted a more than usual number of writers, painters, musicians, actors, and television producers. Oh yes, and poets. Not that I would call them residents. Most of them still live mainly in London and just have second homes in the countryside around Taviscombe. There are a few full-timers as well as Adrian. Oliver Stevens, who makes those marvellous television documentaries, lives in a lovely old rectory between Taviscombe and Taunton and Will Maxwell the successful dramatist lives all the year round in a cottage at the end of a rough track in the middle of Exmoor with no mains water. *That's* what I call being a resident.

'You may be right,' I said. 'Personally I hope we don't commission anything. I'm not very good at modern music. Anyway, we haven't settled anything at all about the programme yet. I suppose we'll have to have a committee meeting soon.'

I sighed. Committee meetings are very much a part of Taviscombe life and are either terminally boring or seething with passion, fury and umbrage. Adrian, needless to say, loved them. Although, as I've said, he had a certain reputation in the literary world, I think he found it much more satisfying to his ego to be a big fish in a little pond, and you could see him positively *basking* in the admiration and deference of some of the other committee members. Sometimes in a meeting I daren't catch my friend Rosemary's eye for fear of laughing.

The Lunch was less terrifying than I had expected. I sat next to Alicia Nash (Adrian was sitting beside the Lord Mayor) and it turned out that her son was at the same boarding school that my son Michael had gone to so we had a lovely gossipy chat about the masters and how they *still* hadn't finished the new science block and how absolutely inedible the food was, so that I forgot to feel nervous. My actual talk went off really very well – the microphones were all right, thank goodness – and people seemed to be listening quite attentively. I enjoyed Alicia Nash's talk. She was very funny and the audience warmed to her. Adrian spoke about his book on Scott Fitzgerald and I have to admit that he did it very well. That's the infuriating thing about Adrian. Just when you've written him off as a pretentious bore he suddenly produces a really excellent piece of work and makes you feel small-minded.

After the talks, as we stood rather self-consciously behind our piles of books, pens at the ready, Adrian said: 'Oh, by the way, did I tell you? I've been made Laurence Meredith's literary executor.'

He looked particularly smug as he said this and with good reason. Laurence Meredith was a distinguished literary figure, a friend of Fitzgerald and Hemingway – though he was English – who had died quite recently at an advanced age. He had known a great many famous people and any biography of him would have an immense readership. To have scooped the pool, as it were, of his literary remains was quite a coup. 'Congratulations!' I said. 'I believe he died in the south of France – will you be going out there? How lovely!'

'The papers have been sent to me by his lawyers so I

have to go through them first and, from what I've been able to see so far, there's some really new and quite exciting stuff there. No doubt,' he continued rather grandly, 'it will be necessary for me to go to the villa at Cap d'Antibes at some point.'

He broke off as a young woman approached him, reverently profferring a copy of his book for his signature, murmuring shyly as she gazed up at him that it was absolutely *marvellous*. I heard a faint snort from Alicia Nash on my other side and smiled. Adrian was never short of young female admirers. I suppose he did look rather like an archetypal poet, tall and thin with dark wavy hair and large dark eyes. He had long, thin hands, too, which he tended to wave about a lot.

Then an elderly woman approached who wanted to tell me that her mother had actually known Ada Leverson and I became so engrossed that I forgot all about Adrian, and everyone else, for that matter.

Driving home I thought about Adrian Palgrave and his wife Enid. She wrote cookery books – well, actually what she did was collect and publish old recipes (which she insisted on calling receipts) some of which sounded pretty revolting, but with a lot of handsome illustrations. The books sold very well, I believe. She was a plain woman in her early forties, a few years older than Adrian, and Taviscombe gossip had it that he only stayed with her (in the face of superior attractions) because 'she had the money'. Like her husband she, too, had a profound sense of her own importance and a tendency to patronize anyone not in her own 'circle', as she put it. I found her a tiresome woman and avoided her when I could, which wasn't easy since she, as well as Adrian, liked to involve herself in local affairs and our paths crossed quite often. She too was actively concerned with the Festival and I knew I'd end up in my usual state of irritation and fury, vowing to have nothing to do with it ever again.

The Taviscombe Festival was held every July. Originally it had been a simple and enjoyable event organized

12

by and for the locals who did the whole thing themselves – all the music, drama, poetry reading, and painting. But in the fullness of time it had inevitably been taken over by Adrian and his friends. They wanted to make it 'more professional' and imported a number of their friends from outside to sing and play and act and put the whole thing, as Enid said, 'on a sound financial footing'. When it reached this stage I had hoped to slide out of the whole affair, but they were very keen to keep local participation (that was Adrian being patronizing again) and so a token number of old Taviscombe residents were kept on the committee. I had protested to my friend Rosemary, but she said, 'Oh, come on Sheila, it'll be good for a laugh. And anyway, *somebody's* got to keep an eye on things or goodness knows what grandiose schemes they'll cook up!'

Actually, in among the junk mail and bills waiting for me when I got home there was a summons to a Festival committee meeting the following week. When I telephoned Rosemary to say that I was back and I'd be round to collect the animals (she always nobly looks after them when I'm away) I asked if she was going to the meeting.

'When is it? Tuesday? I suppose so. Thank the Lord for videos – they always choose a night when there's something I want to watch on the box. I suppose Adrian is too high minded to watch anything but his own programmes and trendy documentaries. How was he? Did he make a mess of his speech?'

'No, actually the speech was very good. *He* was his usual insufferable self though, banging on about commissioning things for the Festival or getting international stars . . .'

'All for the greater glory of Adrian Palgrave. How does he intend to lure them down here, then?'

'He informed me that I underestimate the influence that he and his chums have in Artistic Circles.'

Rosemary laughed.

'You mean he only has to lift his little finger and

13

Menuhin and Pavarotti will drop everything to come to Taviscombe?'

'I don't suppose even he would aim *that* high, but I suppose some of his BBC buddies may rally round. Anyway, we'll doubtless see what delights he has in store for us on Tuesday. Right, then, I'll be round right away to collect Foss and the dogs. I hope they behaved themselves.'

'Bless them, they were very good, as usual. Foss was sick this morning, but I think it was only because he'd been eating grass.'

Later that evening, sitting on the sofa with a dog on either side and Foss on my lap, drinking cocoa and watching *Newsnight* with half an eye, I idly wondered if this year's Festival would *really* be any different from those of previous years.

Chapter Two

'Oh, Sheila, isn't it exciting! Adrian says he may be able to get Leo Spenser to read some of his poems – Adrian's poems, that is – wouldn't that be *thrilling*! I thought he was *marvellous* in that play – you know the one we all went to Bath to see. At the Theatre Royal. Ibsen, was it? Or Chekhov? I always mix them up. But I did think Leo Spenser was absolutely terrific – that bit at the end when he goes mad!'

Eleanor Scott moved towards me with such enthusiasm that half her cup of coffee slopped over into the saucer, something that didn't surprise me at all since she is one of the clumsiest people I know. Who but Eleanor could manage to break her ankle falling *up* the four steps to our local library! She drives me mad in some ways but she is a good-hearted soul and I've always been very fond of her. The Festival Committee meeting was, in fact, taking place in her house. Well, I say house, but it is rather more of a second-league stately home – Kinsford Manor, a large and splendid example of seventeenth-century domestic architecture. Several of the more prestigious events of the Festival usually take place in the Great Hall and that, of course, is why Eleanor is on the committee.

Our committee meeting was being held in what used to be the estate office and there were maps and plans on the walls and a great deal of dark oak furniture. In this very masculine sombre setting Eleanor's bright schoolgirlish chatter seemed out of place. Indeed, at first glance,

15

Eleanor seemed an improbable chatelaine of Kinsford. It was an unusual story. Sir Ernest Barraclough, whose family had lived at Kinsford for generations, had been a widower with one young daughter when Eleanor's parents were killed in an air-crash, leaving her an orphan when she was only nine. Her mother was Sir Ernest's cousin and, since Eleanor had no other close relatives, he had adopted her and brought her to live at Kinsford as a companion for his daughter Phyllis. Tragically, when Phyllis was just twenty-one she died in a sailing accident. And when, some twenty years later, Sir Ernest died, Eleanor inherited the house and the estate. She had never married. The county had hopefully linked her name with those of numerous young men, since she was very definitely a 'catch', but it seemed that even the glories of Kinsford were not enough to compensate for her awkwardness and gauche manner.

'Honestly,' my friend Rosemary said once, when Eleanor was being more than usually Angela Brazil, 'I sometimes wonder if she isn't actually *retarded*!'

'Oh, it's not as bad as that!' I had protested. 'I know she's dreadfully jolly hockey-sticks, but she does mean well.'

But it was rather wearing sometimes, since she tended to attach herself to Rosemary and me as certain girls at school used to do. And, if she never actually *said*, 'Will you be my friend,' as they did, the appeal was there in her large brown eyes.

'Like some beseeching *spaniel*!' Rosemary said. 'Except that I'm devoted to spaniels.'

Still, as I said, I was fond of Eleanor and responded with what I hoped was equal enthusiasm to her news about Leo Spenser.'

'Yes, he is good – such an intelligent actor. I'd like to hear him reading Byron rather than Adrian's stuff, though.'

Eleanor gave me a conspiratorial smile and said, 'Well, actually, I don't really understand Adrian's poems. I'm

16

sure they're awfully *good* – everyone says so – but I really only like poems that rhyme. Oh and Shakespeare, too, though he rhymes sometimes, doesn't he?'

'I wonder how Adrian got hold of someone so prestigious as Leo Spenser?' I asked.

'Oh, I think it was something to do with the BBC.' Eleanor pronounced the initials with reverence. 'I think he said that they were doing a programme together.'

'Oh well,' I said grudgingly, 'full marks to Adrian.'

'What on earth, I wonder, can you be giving our ineffable chairman full marks for?' a voice behind me enquired. It was a very beautiful voice, deep and velvety, carefully produced and nurtured, and used, inflection by inflection, to convey mood and critical evaluation as well as mere information. Will Maxwell had been an actor before he took to writing plays.

'What's ineffable mean?' Eleanor asked.

'Look it up, my dear child, in a dictionary in that great big library of yours.' Will smiled at her kindly. He too was fond of Eleanor, as he was fond of children, animals and other vulnerable creatures. I turned to greet him with pleasure.

'Oh, Will, I'm so glad you managed to come. It's going to be a fairly dire meeting. The Palgrave fan club is here in force and Rosemary and I will need all the help we can get to stop them turning the whole Festival into a three-ringed circus.'

'If only they would,' Will said. 'Adrian as ring-master, of course, in a top hat, cracking a whip, with all the others jumping through hoops. Now that I would pay money to see.'

'Eleanor says that Adrian thinks he can get hold of Leo Spenser, but unfortunately he will be reading Adrian's poems.'

'Never mind, darling,' Will grinned. 'You can always close your ears and just *gaze*.'

'Yes, well, it does seem such a waste.' I turned to

17

Eleanor and asked, 'Is Father Freddy going to be here tonight?'

'No. Such a shame – it's a meeting of the PCC. He had to be there, of course, and the dates clashed.'

The Reverend Frederic Drummond was the rector of the beautiful church, whose great sandstone tower we could see from the window. St Decumen's has a very fine organ (restored and improved by the benefaction of Sir Ernest) and a large and impressive interior so that the church, in addition to its more ecclesiastical function, is always greatly in demand for concerts. The Rector himself is equally impressive – tall and powerfully built. Even now, in his late seventies, he's a formidable figure. Like some great ruined oak, Will used to say. At Oxford, and later in London, he had been part of that Bohemian literary society that features so often nowadays in memoirs and biographies. Even after he had taken orders he was usually to be found in fairly exclusive circles and his churches were always in the most fashionable square mile of London. He's marvellous company with a fund of splendid stories and he still tackles everything with tremendous gusto – food, drink, friendship, life. His parishioners are very proud of him (though the greater part of his conversation with them might just as well be in a foreign language), as they might be of some exotic bird that had chosen to land in their back gardens. St Decumen's has had a tradition in recent years of having elderly retired clergyman – it is, everyone feels, much better than being amalgamated with three or four other parishes – but they had previously been retired service chaplains, whose style and force of delivery were more generally suited to the quarter-deck or a windy parade ground. Compared with them, Father Freddy (as even the villagers called him) was a *rara avis* indeed. I was sorry he wouldn't be at this meeting since his ironic eye and unclerical asides usually provide me with much-needed relief.

Will took Eleanor's coffee cup, which was sliding dangerously off its saucer.

'Allow me.' He turned to me. 'Can I fetch you another cup?'

'No, thanks. I'll have one afterwards when we're allowed to get at all that delicious food. You know,' I added, 'I only came on to this committee so that I could enjoy Jessie's heavenly shrimp patties.' Jessie was Eleanor's housekeeper and a fabulous cook. With typical generosity, Eleanor always provided a substantial buffet supper on committee evenings and it was certainly the most agreeable part of the evening for all but the most egotistical committee members.

'You're right,' Will said. 'I'll go and chivvy Adrian to make a start – the sooner we begin, the sooner we'll finish and get down to the real business of the evening.'

I watched with affection his tall, thin figure moving purposefully across the room. I've known Will for years – ever since he first came down here and bought that remote cottage after his wife died tragically young in a road accident. He's had the most tremendous success and recently critics have begun to call him a classic comic writer, which, he says, makes him feel very old. But a new Will Maxwell play is always a theatrical event and his rare television scripts are as notable for their excellence as for their popular appeal. Since Peter died he has been very kind, giving me dinner occasionally or, if we happen to be in London at the same time, taking me to the theatre. Though going to the theatre with Will is not unalloyed pleasure. He fidgets in what he feels to be the badly written bits or startles his neighbour in the adjoining seat by a sharp, very audible intake of breath when the author has achieved some technical feat of which he approves.

Enid Palgrave, looking, as I said to Rosemary afterwards, more like a hobbit than ever, suddenly appeared and said rather rudely, I thought, since it *was* Eleanor's house, 'Come along, now, you two. All this coffee and chatter is all very well, but we really must get started!'

I raised my eyebrows at this peremptory tone but Eleanor, who appears to regard Enid as a sort of Head

Girl figure, said, 'Oh, so sorry, Enid. Where do you want us to sit?'

I gravitated towards Rosemary who was talking to young Robin Turner, our Treasurer. Robin is a very nice boy who works in Jack's firm of accountants. He's desperately shy and has recently had a sort of nervous breakdown. Rosemary and her husband Jack befriended him and it was Rosemary who persuaded him to be the Festival Treasurer (a thankless task and one for which there are never any volunteers) in the hope that it might 'take him out of himself'. He manages the financial side of things beautifully, being one of those people who are more at home with figures than with people, but the prospect of actually having to get up and speak at a meeting fills him with terror and he can only manage it if Rosemary is close at hand to cheer him on.

I gave him what I hoped was an encouraging smile.

'Hello, Robin, hello, Rosemary. Shall we all sit together? Then we can have a little giggle if Adrian is too impossible.'

The meeting went on and on, as meetings do. Every item was discussed, turned inside out, and discussed all over again. I suppressed a yawn and looked surreptitiously at my watch, looked up and caught Will's eye. He winked at me. Various people expressed surprise that various other people didn't agree with them. Umbrage was taken. My thoughts drifted away and I found myself wondering how anyone, even Enid Palgrave, could have actually *chosen* a blouse in that relentlessly unbecoming shade of mustard.

A sharp interchange roused me from my abstraction. Adrian was being thoroughly unpleasant to poor Robin. Something to do with the allocation of funds.

'But the money simply isn't *there* for such a project,' Robin was saying doggedly. 'If we haven't got it, we can't spend it.'

'This is absolutely intolerable!' Adrian was being his most high-handed and infuriating. 'It is not for you to say what this committee can or cannot do.'

20

Robin tried to answer but Adrian didn't draw breath but went on and on, becoming more and more unpleasant and sarcastic. It's always the same – anyone who opposes him is usually talked down in this way. Most people are used to it; they simply shrug and go round about and get things done some other way. But poor Robin obviously couldn't cope. His face was flushed and he seemed almost in tears. Rosemary tried to protest and so did Will but Adrian in full flow is difficult to stop. Robin suddenly got to his feet.

'I'm not going to listen to any more of this! You're hateful and unfair and I won't stay here to be bullied by you like this.'

Robin was definitely in tears now and his voice as he threw the childish phrase at Adrian was verging on the hysterical. He snatched up the pile of papers in front of him and, overturning his chair in his haste, he almost ran from the room. There was an embarrassed silence then Rosemary got up.

'Well, Adrian, I hope you're proud of yourself, picking on the poor boy like that. I'd better go and see if he's all right.'

Adrian looked around the table but no one met his eye.

'Oh, for goodness' sake!' he said. 'If the boy can't argue things out rationally! So emotional and unbalanced!'

Will went and picked up the overturned chair.

'What a disagreeable schoolboy you must have been, Adrian,' he said. 'I expect you pulled the wings off flies as well.'

Enid shot him a poisonous look.

'Mr Chairman, I propose we get on with the meeting,' she said. 'There are still a great many things to be decided and I for one do not have time to waste.'

The meeting did continue, but the atmosphere was sour and even more squabbles than usual broke out. Eventually Adrian realized that nothing useful was going to be decided and closed the whole thing down much earlier than usual.

It was with some relief that we all moved into another room for the refreshments. Tables had been set out in the morning room, piled with plates and bowls of food. Jessie quickly set to work to dish out potato salad and Coronation Chicken and the famous shrimp patties. Jessie is Welsh, a large, handsome woman, with the typical dark hair and high colouring and just a faint lilt in her voice. I suppose she must be in her mid-thirties now. She came straight from an orphanage at sixteen to work at Kinsford and is deeply devoted to Miss Eleanor, as she has always insisted on calling her.

'Hello, Jessie,' I said. 'I've been looking forward to this all day!'

She smiled with pleasure. I thought how attractive she was and wondered why she had never married.

'Good evening, Mrs Malory, it's very nice of you to say so. Have some of this avocado dip. It's a new recipe I found in one of those books at the hairdresser's.'

'It looks gorgeous. What a pity Father Freddy isn't here tonight to try it!'

'Oh, the Reverend does enjoy his food. It's a real pleasure to cook for him.'

'He certainly does! Last time he came to see me he ate a whole *plateful* of coconut pyramids!'

We smiled together, the old-fashioned smile of two women who do like to see a man eat.

With my plate satisfactorily filled I looked around the room. Only Adrian's two most enthusiastic supporters, Geraldine Marwick and Evelyn Page, were talking to him and Enid. Everyone else, though not exactly shunning him, were contriving to be in some other part of the room. The general feeling seemed to be that this time Adrian really had gone too far. Rosemary came in and I went over to see how Robin was.

'He's gone home,' she said. 'I got him calmed down a bit so that he was okay to drive, but he wanted to go and, honestly, I really don't think he could bear to be in the same room with Adrian after that.'

22

'Oh dear,' I said. 'Poor boy! Does that mean he'll resign?'

'Oh yes, he was quite firm about that. It was the last straw, really. Adrian's always been foul to him – he wanted Geraldine to be Treasurer, you know.'

'But she's practically innumerate!' I exclaimed.

'Yes, but she's one of his buddies. Robin was far too good and conscientious to suit Adrian. You weren't at last month's meeting, were you? He and Enid between them criticised every single item of Robin's financial report – it was terribly embarrassing and awful for Robin, who'd done a really good job. I was absolutely seething!'

'Someone should strangle them both,' I said. 'Anyway, you've done what you can – come and get some food.'

We moved over to the table where Eleanor was talking to Jessie. She looked distressed and said, 'I know Adrian is very clever and all that, but I do think he was absolutely beastly to poor Robin! I hate it when people are sarcastic like that. Where is Robin?' she asked Rosemary.

'He's gone home. He was very upset.'

'Poor thing, I'm not surprised. It was dreadful – I hate scenes and arguments.'

Her face was grave and she spoke with an unusual intensity. Then Jessie asked Rosemary about the food she wanted and the conversation became more general. After a short while Enid came up to Eleanor and, ignoring Rosemary and me, said, 'I'm afraid we have to dash, Eleanor, dear. Adrian needs an early night – he has to be up at crack of dawn to get the train to London. Rehearsals for his new poetry programme, you know. So do forgive us if we just slip away. Thanks for your splendid hospitality!'

She turned and collected Adrian and swept him out of the room all in one movement.

Rosemary snorted.

'At least *she* could see that they weren't exactly flavour of the month just now. Not that she's much better than he is – bossy cow!'

Eleanor giggled. 'Oh, Rosemary, what a dreadful thing to say!'

'Well, she is. And patronizing. And dreary. At least Adrian can be amusing in a catty sort of way. She's just sourdough.'

'What exactly *is* sourdough?' I asked, wishing to turn the subject since Eleanor was still looking upset. 'Do you know, Jessie? I'm sure I've seen something about sourdough rolls in an American cookery book.'

Jessie paused in her attempt to fill Rosemary's plate to overflowing and considered the question.

'I couldn't really say, Mrs Malory. I suppose it might be a bread dough made with sour milk. Like scones, you know. I should think it would be very nice.'

Will came to join us.

'Can I have some of that exquisite trifle, Jessie?' he asked. 'I feel I can eat more freely now that the termites have gone.'

'Termites, would you say?' I considered the word. 'I'd thought weevils, but you may be right – or *lower* than vermin, perhaps.'

'The hand of God reaching down into the slime,' Will quoted with relish, 'couldn't raise *them* to the depths of degradation.'

Eleanor, who had been swivelling from Will to me like a Wimbledon fan, said, 'Oh I do love listening to you two! It's as good as a play!'

'A Will Maxwell play, of course,' he said.

I laughed. 'I'm very flattered that I'm considered worthy of speaking your dialogue!'

Now that the Palgraves had gone, shortly followed by their two henchwomen, the whole atmosphere was lighter and more frivolous, almost like a party. Little knots of people ate and chatted and laughed and practically no one mentioned the Festival.

Eleanor was in her element; she was a great one for entertaining. There were not many grand parties now, as there had been in Sir Ernest's time. He had been in

24

the Foreign Office and in his heyday there had been entertaining on a very grand scale indeed. Eleanor and Phyllis had been schoolgirls then, of course, and after Phyllis' death Sir Ernest had almost severed his links with the greater world outside. There were still gatherings at Kinsford, but they were of local people, and as he and Eleanor drew together in grief at her death there were fewer even of these. After Sir Ernest had died Eleanor had gone abroad for some months and when she returned she had thrown herself energetically into local events, opening up Kinsford for every one of the fund-raisers who had approached her.

When I went to say goodbye I said, 'Thank you for a lovely party!'

'It was fun, wasn't it, after – you know.'

'Yes. I'm sorry poor Robin missed the good bit. We'll have to find something else in the Festival for him to do, something that doesn't involve horrible Adrian.'

'Oh yes, what a good idea. Why don't you and Rosemary come to tea next week and we'll try and think of something? I'm sure there's a job that's just right for him. Cousin Ernest always used to say that there is a round hole for every round peg if only you look long enough.'

Eleanor had the habit of quoting some of Sir Ernest's more tedious clichés as if they were Holy Writ. In other people it might have been profoundly irritating, in Eleanor Rosemary and I found it rather touching. She still missed him very much and tried to keep Kinsford as much as possible as it had been when he was still alive. I often felt that her deep involvement in local affairs was something that she did for his sake since, in spite of her jolly manner, she was, underneath, a shy person. But if it was what he would have wished, a family responsibility, then she would do it, whatever the cost to herself. There was something rather splendid about her dedication to his memory which made one respect her in spite of her gaucheness and occasionally aggravating ways.

'That would be lovely, Nell,' I said warmly, using the

diminutive of our younger days. 'I'll organize Rosemary and fix a day. Thank you so much for everything. See you soon.'

As I walked down the drive to where I had left my car Will came up behind me.

'Are you OK? Do you want a torch?'

'No, I'm fine, it's a lovely moonlit night. Just look at the stars!'

We paused for a moment to stare up at the soft black sky above us decorated with an uncountable number of glittering points of light. 'Goodness,' I said, 'aren't we lucky to live in the country!'

Will drew my arm through his.

'Come along, let me lead you to your car before you fall into a ditch looking at the stars.'

We walked companionably together and Will said, 'Was Robin all right?'

'Rosemary calmed him down, I think. But he's resigned.'

'Adrian really ought to be boiled *very* slowly in oil.'

'Do you think he has any sort of human feelings?' I asked.

'It would seem unlikely. His nature is irredeemably cold.'

'Not even for Enid?'

'Can you *imagine* anyone having any human feelings for Enid? Apart from profound dislike. Nor do I imagine that *she* has any human feelings either, so they are perfectly matched. What was it that someone said about how fortunate it was that the Carlyles married each other so that two people were made miserable instead of four.'

'So unreasonable,' I protested, 'I'm devoted to Jane Carlyle – think of those heavenly letters! Do you remember her saying that when she got out of the train after a journey she looked and felt as if she had just returned from the Thirty Years War? How well one knows the feeling!'

He laughed.

'Travel by train has, if anything, deteriorated since the 1840s. Come, let me shine the torch while you look for your car keys. Why do women always fill their handbags with all that impedimenta? Yours is quite as large as Miss Prism's and could easily accommodate the manuscript of a three-volume novel.'

I opened the door of my car.

'Will you be at the next meeting?' I asked.

'I suppose so. Having put my hand to the plough and all that.'

'Well, I'll see you then.'

'Oh, before that.' He leaned on the bonnet of the car and lit his pipe. 'I've just finished the first draft of a new television play and will need a certain amount of comfort and reassurance. So do, please, say that you'll have dinner with me next week. Friday?'

'Yes please, I'd love to. And by then Rosemary, Eleanor, and I may have thought how to find another Festival job for Robin.'

He made sucking, gurgling noises with his pipe and said, 'I shall await events with the utmost eagerness. I'll ring you.'

He shut the car door for me and was gone.

As I drove home my headlights picked out a small rabbit at the side of the road, its eyes fixed and mesmerized by the light. I slowed down, just in case it felt like dashing out and committing suicide under my wheels, and I thought of poor Robin, and hoped that Adrian's brutal behaviour hadn't made him withdraw completely into his neurotic shell. And then I thought about what Will had said about Adrian's lack of feelings and wondered, as I often did, whether, behind the façade of polite joviality, Will had allowed himself to indulge in the luxury of feelings once again. He was friendly and caring and compassionate to those in trouble, but there seemed no way of telling what if anything lay beneath, and what his thoughts were as he sat alone in the dark, low-ceilinged study in his cottage, so far from any other human

27

habitation. But, as always, search as I might for some clue in his conversation, I was no nearer a conclusion than I had been on the day before my husband's funeral, when Will had gently taken my hand and I had sobbed away a part of my grief while he remained white-faced and silent.

Chapter Three

The scent of Brompton stocks in the flowerbed round the statue of Queen Anne in the Square made me suddenly decide to go to the garden centre to get the bedding plants. Mr Chapman, who comes once a week to see to my garden and who, over the years, has established the sort of tyrannical power that such essential people wield, had been recently making noises about the need to get on with the planting out. He is a splendid man and wonderful with vegetables but his idea of a nicely planted bed is a rigid row of orange tagetes, backed by a parallel row of cerise petunias, the whole thing finished off in fine military fashion by a guardsman-straight row of scarlet salvias. Consequently I always tried to get the annuals bought and planted when he was safely out of the way. I had loaded my trolley with the usual lobelia and alyssum and had gone mad among the new varieties of asters, nicotiana and some very exciting curly-edged petunias, had splurged dreadfully among the pelargoniums and impatiens and had decided that I simply couldn't live through the summer without a dozen new fuchsias, and was, as a result, feeling a little dazed by my own extravagance. I came to rest in the section of the garden centre devoted to garden ornaments. I had admired and coveted a couple of massive urns, rioting with vine and acanthus leaves, and was just wondering what sort of person it might be who would buy a representation of an old boot lovingly moulded in concrete, when a voice behind me said, 'Now don't tell me, Sheila darling, that you are proposing to buy that excessively coy-looking rabbit!'

It was Oliver Stevens. He is a large man, over six feet tall, and what, if you wished to be polite, you might call well-built. He looked even bulkier than usual in a heavy Aran sweater and corduroys and, with his round face and his beard, looked very like the popular conception of Henry VIII. He is an amiable man, liked by all. We locals were a little wary of him at first – a *television* producer – we didn't know quite what to expect – but his friendly manner and good-natured willingness to join in everything without any side or affectation made him universally popular. The only fly in the ointment ('And wouldn't you know that there'd have to be one?' as Rosemary said) was his wife. Sally Stevens, although now in her forties, is still a wide-eyed fluffy blonde with a girlish laugh and a tiresome 'little-me' manner. She's also very county – actually I think her parents did have some sort of quite grand country house somewhere in Norfolk (Sally gave the impression that it was rather larger than Chatsworth or Blenheim) but I don't think there was a lot of money. She's very into hunting and horses and the Stevens' Range Rover always has a couple of hysterical Jack Russells barking their heads off.

I imagine it was for Sally that Oliver had bought the rather beautiful Georgian rectory with its stables and paddocks since he himself remains incurably urban. He loves the theatre, opera, expensive London restaurants, and generally being at the heart of things, as he says. As well as being a successful television producer he also writes film scripts and the occasional novel. He's very successful in all these fields – which is just as well for the Stevens' life style must be very expensive – but he has a huge talent which matches his great gusto for life and for all the good things it offers. Since his work mostly keeps him in London throughout the week he has a small flat ('In dear old Knightsbridge, darling, among the jolly old Arabs') which must be a convenient bolt-hole when he wants to escape from Sally. It's obvious to the most casual observer that although for Oliver the marriage is only a polite convention, Sally is a fiercely possessive wife. Even now, as I turned to speak to Oliver, she appeared as if from nowhere and thrust her arm through his, giving him what I suppose she imagined was a winsome smile.

'*There* you are, darling,' she said. 'I couldn't see *where* you'd got to! I want you to come and look at those stone slabs for the terrace.'

She turned to me and said condescendingly, 'How nice to see you, Sheila. Are you getting a few plants for your little garden? They really have quite a good selection here, though *we* always order ours when we go to Chelsea. It's such fun to have the newest varieties, don't you think?'

'Yes,' I said colourlessly, 'great fun.'

Oliver gave me a quizzical look.

'By the way,' he said, 'what do think about Adrian's luck in getting hold of the Meredith papers? Jammy bastard! There should be a couple of books and a telly programme in it for him at the very least!'

'I know,' I replied. 'He's very full of it. I believe he'll do the collected letters first and then the *Life* – that's the easy way round, isn't it? And I'm sure he'll do a radio programme as well. Perhaps you would do the television one.'

'I don't think I could bear to work with Adrian on a programme again – not after that thing we did on Lytton Strachey. He argued over every single comma in the script. I really couldn't be doing with that sort of thing again. I wouldn't mind doing something about Meredith myself, but I bet he won't release any of the material to anyone else, seeing that he has the copyright. He's a miserable sod!'

'I'm afraid you're right,' I replied. 'Goodness knows one is used to practically everyone in the literary world clutching their little bits of material jealously to their bosoms, but there's a sort of mean-mindedness about him that I find extremely rebarbative.'

Sally, who had been showing signs of restiveness

throughout a conversation in which she had played no part, said in a whiny voice, 'Ollie, I'm getting *cold* and we really ought to be getting on. Remember we're having lunch with the Howards.' She glanced sharply at me as she said this to see how I would react to the name of the Lord Lieutenant of the county.

'Oh, don't fuss, Sally,' he replied comfortably, 'there's masses of time and I never seem to see Sheila nowadays to have a good chat.'

I gave Sally what I hoped was a gracious smile and, grasping the handle of my loaded trolley, said, 'Actually, I should be getting on myself. I must get all these things planted out before my gardener comes tomorrow and the forecast said it's going to rain this afternoon. Anyway, I'll probably be seeing you around during the Festival, one always runs into everyone there!'

'Oh God, yes! Madrigals and morris dancing and local art.'

'Worse than that – readings of Adrian's poetry and a talk by Antonia Basset about the social relevance of the novel in the post-Thatcher era.'

Oliver groaned. Antonia Basset, the well-known Hampstead intellectual, had recently bought a second home just outside Taviscombe and was now a part of the Adrian Palgrave circle and thus liable to be trotted out as a speaker on every cultural occasion. I used to like her novels when they were full of undergraduate energy, but now that she's gone in for soggy sociology to the tune of five hundred pages a book I really do find her unreadable. She is probably rather nice underneath, I suspect, but can't help taking herself dreadfully seriously as a Novelist or – even worse – a Writer. When, in her first Little Talk, she spoke in Wordsworthian tones about how she gathered Inspiration for her novels by Wandering about the Country Lanes, Rosemary disgraced herself badly by giving a great snort of laughter and I must say I didn't dare to meet her eye.

'Let me know when that will be, dear heart,' Oliver said, 'and I will arrange to be in London.'

I laughed and, waving goodbye, trundled my trolley out into the carpark.

Time passed quickly, as it always does in the summer months – it's extraordinary how slowly time passes in the winter – and my son Michael finished his last term at the College of Law in London and came home to bite his nails, waiting for the result of his Finals.

'It's not that it isn't *marvellous* to have you here, darling,' I said one morning when he had told me for the fourth time that he *knew* he had screwed up his Tax and Inheritance paper, 'but why don't you go down and stay with Ron and Eva? Tom and Felicity will be home from Cambridge now and I'm sure it would be more amusing for you to get out and about a bit with them, rather than sit mooching around the house here.'

'No, I don't think so.' He was sitting at the breakfast table, with his chair precariously tilted back, making patterns in the butter with a crumby knife. 'I wouldn't *enjoy* myself, not knowing, and that would be depressing for them.'

I bit back the obvious remark and said tentatively, 'Well, you know that Edward did say that if you would like to go into the office for a bit, just to get some work experience before you start, he'd be very glad to have you.'

Edward Drayton had been Peter's partner and Michael was due to start with him in the autumn as an articled clerk.

'You might just as well have something positive to do to take your mind off things. Then when you get your results, you can have a good holiday before you start in September.'

Michael, who appeared to be concentrating on engraving a fleur-de-lis in the butter, said dejectedly, '*If* I pass. Otherwise I'll be doing retakes all summer.'

'Well,' I said brightly, 'why don't you give Edward a ring and see if he can take you for a few weeks.'

'OK, Ma. It's really quite a good idea. I'll ring him now.'

He gave me a sudden cheerful smile and got up briskly from the table, letting the knife, which was now covered with butter as well as crumbs, fall on to the clean tablecloth. He came back into the kitchen while I was cutting up some liver for the animals and said, 'Brilliant. He's asked me to go in on Monday. I think I'll take the dogs for a walk.'

There was a scuffle of paws on parquet, a cheerful shout, a slammed door, and he was gone. Foss, who had ignored all the commotion, concentrating his very being on the business in hand, gave a loud and scornful wail and continued to weave around the chopping board on the work-top.

As the time for the Festival approached I realized that I must take my velvet skirt to be cleaned. It was a convention (Adrian's idea, of course, and no one had the strength to oppose him) that the committee should wear evening dress for the more formal occasions and the opening concert at Kinsford – this year it was to be a very famous early English consort playing madrigals and lute music – was the most formal of all. I scrabbled through my wardrobe in the vain hope that I might find some wonderfully suitable garment that I had forgotten, but, as I knew I would, I came back to my black velvet skirt, which was the only long one I possessed. It was pretty old and had done valiant service over the years, being long and voluminous enough to hide the woollen underwear and heavy stockings that are essential wear in some of the more underheated houses of the neighbourhood.

I held it up to the light and sighed. It was obvious that at some time it had fallen off its hanger and had then been slept on by Foss, since it was crumpled and covered in cat hairs. I shook it vigorously and bundled it up in a plastic bag, hoping that dry cleaning would perform some sort of miracle upon it.

I was just coming out of the cleaner's when I was nearly run down by Rosemary, who was inexpertly propelling her granddaughter in a push-chair.

'Isn't it awful,' she said, 'how you forget how to do these things. I still haven't got the knack, especially getting up and down the kerbs.' I made friendly overtures to the small person bundled up in an anorak in the push-chair and she responded with an enchanting smile and the offer of a half-chewed biscuit.

'Hasn't she *grown*!' I said inanely, but it really is amazing how small children do double in size when you haven't seen them for a few weeks. 'Are both Jilly and Roger with you?'

'Well, Jilly's here now and Roger will be coming next week. He's got a few days' leave and says he's got a thing about madrigals and would like to come to the opening Festival do.'

'How lovely! I'll look forward to seeing them.'

Jilly is my god-daughter and I'm also very fond of her husband, Roger, who is a police inspector in the CID and, surprisingly (though I don't know why I should think so), a passionate devotee of Victorian literature. I indicated Rosemary's granddaughter who was now leaning perilously out of her push-chair attempting to unscrew one of the wheels.

'And what about Delia?'

'Oh, Jack will baby-sit. His musical tastes don't go much beyond Frank Sinatra and Nat King Cole. Anyway, he can't bear most of the Festival people. Oh well, I'd better get on. Mother's got the hairdresser coming this morning and she needs some special sort of *biscuit* that she likes to give her with her coffee!'

Rosemary has a difficult mother who keeps her running round in circles and is the reason for her permanently harassed expression.

'Poor you,' I said sympathetically. 'Tell Jilly I'd love to see her if she can find a moment. I'll give you a ring some time before next week. I saw Eleanor yesterday; I thought she looked a bit peaky. I hope she isn't sickening for something. She says she *thinks* everything's going smoothly, but there's always some sort of last-minute hitch. Remember last year, when that *Lieder* singer fell asleep on the train and got carried on to Plymouth!'

I decided that the only way to retrieve the black velvet skirt was to buy a new, eye-catching blouse and made my way to Taviscombe's one and only dress shop, Estelle's. Estelle herself, a small woman of uncertain age, heavily made-up and with a kind of ruthless chic, was selling a short pillar-box red jacket to a bemused farmer's wife who had wandered in to have a look round and had been trapped by Estelle's mesmerizing sales-talk. I slunk round to the rails at the back and was just about to go into the fitting room with a pretty flowery blue blouse, rather low-cut and with a frill down the front, when a hand snatched it away from me and Estelle's sharp voice said, 'Oh *no*, Mrs Malory! That isn't you at *all*.'

'I really wanted something a bit dressy to perk up an old black skirt,' I said feebly.

'*Dressy*!' There was a world of scorn in her voice. 'A black skirt?' She pawed briskly through the garments on the rail and thrust into my arms a severely cut black and white blouse with a high neck and long sleeves. And of course she was right – when I looked in the mirror I felt almost elegant. And of *course*, it was hideously expensive, nearly twice as much as the one I'd first chosen. Estelle had won again, but I didn't begrudge her the victory. I reckoned I owed it to my morale to look just a little dashing on this particular occasion.

Secure in the glory of my new finery I sat in the Great Hall at Kinsford looking about me. The panelled walls are hung with portraits and I was sitting beside one of Sir Ernest. It had been done in the fifties by James Gunn and showed Sir Ernest, I suppose, in his prime. He had chosen to be painted in evening dress with some exotic-looking order hung round his neck, a relic, presumably of one of his diplomatic tours of duty. He was leaning, a tall, elegant figure, on the balustrade that ran around the terrace at Kinsford, with the lake in the background – a classical pose. I had always felt, on the occasions when I met Sir Ernest, that he was almost too good to be true.

Children usually sense these things. So that although he had been the perfect father and guardian at Phyllis and Eleanor's parties (he had always made a point of being there for them if he possibly could), organizing the games and superintending the lavish teas with genial good humour, it seemed to me that he was standing outside himself, observing the effect he was having on other people, even on small children. Now, as the light set over the portrait picked out the cold grey stare, I decided I had not been mistaken. The Hall was looking really beautiful. The lights gleamed on the dark panels and reflected the shine of the silvery-grey brocade curtains hanging at the shuttered windows. Great bowls of flowers stood on tables and in alcoves – Eleanor has a real talent for such things and always does the most wonderful arrangements for the St Decumen's Flower Festival. As well as portraits, the walls are hung with ancient weapons and banners which draw the eye up to the glorious plaster-work of the ceiling.

I looked at Eleanor, whose dress featured immense splashes of scarlet poppies on a black ground and made her look enormous, dashing about heartily shaking people's hands and generally being a good hostess. She looked flushed and excited, anxious that everything should go well. She had Robin at her side. Typically, after the unpleasant interlude with Adrian, she had taken him under her wing and made him her Man Friday (lots of little jokes about this) and certainly he seemed to be looking much more cheerful and sure of himself, following her about as she greeted newcomers and chatted with old friends. Perhaps that was the solution for both of them, I thought – a mother figure for him and a child substitute for her. I looked around for Rosemary to tell her about my inspiration but she was at the other end of the row. Committee members sat in the front two rows, except for Adrian who always liked to sit at the back ('So that I can get out quickly if I'm *needed* for anything').

I twisted round to look at the body of the Hall and

spotted Jilly and Roger, who waved when they saw me, and Sally, sitting on her own. She was all done up very unsuitably in low-cut pale blue chiffon (I blessed Estelle's good taste that had saved me from a similar lapse) and looked very sulky. As I watched, Oliver came in. He seemed rather agitated about something, perhaps Sally's mood, since he was easy-going and hated any sort of unpleasantness and Sally was, as I knew from experience, perfectly capable of making a scene if she was in a bad mood, something that Oliver found deeply embarrassing.

Enid, in fierce electric blue with a lot of pearls, came in and sat with Geraldine and Evelyn, and they were joined by Father Freddy, a magnificent cassocked figure, who nearly extinguished Geraldine as he flung off his long clerical cloak with a theatrical gesture.

The main lights had been switched off, leaving only two great lamps for the performers at one end of the Hall, when Will slipped into the seat on the end of the row beside me.

'Got stuck behind a horse box,' he whispered as the players and singers came in. 'Sorry I'm late.'

The murmurings died away as one of the musicians struck the first light, metallic notes of the lute and the clear voices filled the Hall.

> 'Hold fast now in thy youth,
> Regard thy vowed Truth,
> Lest when thou waxeth old
> Friends fail and Love grows cold.'

Each note seemed to fall separately on the air and I was caught up, as I always am, enchanted by that incomparable blending of words and music.

> 'It is the face of death that smiles,
> Pleasing though it kills the whiles,
> Where death and love in pretty wiles
> Each other mutually beguiles.'

Formal verse that hides deep feeling always moves me and I was aware that Will, sitting beside me was tense and strained.

'My thoughts hold mortal strife.
I do detest my life,
And with lamenting cries
Peace to my soul to bring
Oft call that prince which here doth monarchize:
—But he, grim grinning King,
Who caitiffs scorns, and doth the blest surprise,
Late having deck'd with beauty's rose his tomb,
Disdains to crop a weed, and will not come.'

I wondered if ever, alone in the middle of the night, in the weeks after Lucy's death, Will had ever been tempted to follow her. She had been some years younger than him and in the natural course of events he might have expected to die before her. I glanced at his face, scarcely visible in the dim light and was astonished to see that he was silently weeping.

'All our pride is but a jest;
None are worst and none are best.
Grief and joy and hope and fear
Play their pageants everywhcre;
Vain opinion all doth sway,
And the world is but a play.'

The lights were switched on and I came back reluctantly into the world again. Will muttered something about having a word with Eleanor and hurried away and I slowly rose to my feet and moved towards the far door, easing my way through the crowds of people all making for the refreshments. A great feature of the Festival opening concert was the elaborate cold buffet, subsidized by Eleanor and mostly cooked by Jessie, though other ex-cellent women did contribute flans and gateaux, quiches and the inevitable Coronation Chicken. The money raised went to swell the Festival funds and was one of its main sources of income. The food was laid out in the old kitchen, an immense, high-ceilinged room with an antique range at one end and a stone-flagged floor. Sir Ernest, who cared greatly for his creature comforts, had, however, caused a kitchen, handsomely fitted with every modern device, to be built in the small morning room next to the dining room, thereby ensuring a contented cook and warm food.

Although it was a lovely summer evening, the passage leading to the kitchen was cold and I shivered slightly in my blouse, glad of the long sleeves. In recognition of the importance of the food, the interval was an hour in length so I thought I'd wait a little until the crowd had subsided and walked back into the main body of the house and thence into the garden. It was delightful to be out in the evening air. The scent from the masses of pinks which filled the beds at the side of the house was warm and spicy. Other people were strolling along the paths of the formal garden which led down to the lake, but I didn't follow them. I knew from bitter experience that the mosquitoes were especially active down by the water. Instead I thought I would go and look at the new herb garden that Eleanor had told me she was making in the kitchen courtyard. This was a charming brick-paved area leading out from the kitchen passage and surrounded by old stone outbuildings. Eleanor had created a splendid effect with two seventeenth-century decorated lead cistern filled with flowers and beautifully laid out beds of herbs. I was just bending down to smell a particularly handsome rosemary when Jessie suddenly appeared from one of the buildings. There was obviously something very wrong because she was so agitated that for a moment she didn't see me at all. She had pulled the door behind her and stood leaning back against it; she seemed to be trembling. As I went towards her and she became aware that she wasn't alone, she gave a startled cry. 'Jessie – what on *earth* is the matter?' I asked. 'You look dreadful. What's happened?'

She gave a little shuddering sigh, as if of relief, when she recognized me, and straightening up said, almost in her normal voice, 'Oh, Mrs Malory, thank goodness it is you. I was afraid it might be Miss Eleanor and she mustn't go in there and see – it would upset her so.' Her voice trembled and she broke off, looking at me as if waiting to be told what to do next.

'Jessie, please, what has *happened*? Is it an accident? Is someone hurt?'

'It's Mr Adrian,' she said, 'in there, in the old dairy.'

She stood aside and I opened the door. Although it was still light outside it was dark in the old dairy, and I groped for the switch. The room was flooded with a cold harsh light from the single bulb with its white china shade hanging from the ceiling. The air struck cold since the window was small and let in very little sun, the floor was of stone and the great marble slabs that had once held the bowls of milk and cream seemed to intensify the chill. The place was now used as a store and the shelves, which went all round the room, were piled with plates and great vegetable dishes and tureens, relics of grand dinner parties of the past. I moved a few steps forward and then I saw, beyond some furniture under dust sheets, someone sitting on a chair at the far end of the room. Jessie was still standing in the doorway so I called out, 'Adrian? Is that you? Are you all right?'

I went towards the seated figure and then stopped in horror. It was Adrian, but he was dead: someone had hit him repeatedly on the back of the head, there were terrible gashes, and blood – such a lot of blood.

Chapter Four

I had instinctively closed my eyes, to blot out, I suppose, what I could not bear to look at. The smell of blood has always made me feel sick and as I stood behind the chair where Adrian's body lay slumped I could smell the blood, oozing from those dreadful wounds, matting and darkening the light brown hair, I felt a rising wave of nausea. I turned abruptly away and faced Jessie, saying in a voice I tried to make steady, 'He's obviously dead – there's nothing we can do.'

'Miss Eleanor,' she said urgently. 'She mustn't see this . . .'

'No,' I replied soothingly, 'there's no need. I'll find Roger – Inspector Eliot – he is a policeman and a friend of mine. He'll know what needs to be done.'

Jessie glanced once more at the dead man, an almost casual glance, one more of curiosity than of horror. I wished I had her stoicism. As I closed the door behind us, a thought struck me.

'We ought not to leave it like this. Can we lock it? Is there a key?'

Jessie opened the door again and took a heavy iron key that was on the inside of the door and turned it in the lock. Then she put the key in my hand, as if with it she was also giving me the responsibility for doing whatever had to be done.

As we went towards the house she suddenly said, 'I never got those plates.'

'What plates?' I asked stupidly.

'When we were dishing out the food, it was. Miss Eleanor said, "Jessie, we're running out of plates." So I said I'd go and get some from the old dairy. That's what I came out for. They'll be needing them by now – people won't be able to have their supper and Miss Eleanor will be wondering where on earth I've got to.'

She made as if to go towards the kitchen but I caught hold of her arm.

'No, Jessie, you must come with me. You found the – you found Mr Palgrave and Inspector Eliot will want you to go back with him to the dairy. He'll want to talk to you.'

She seemed reluctant but I pushed her before me into the house and fortunately came across Roger almost at once. He was talking to Rosemary and Jilly as they queued for their refreshments. I found that I was clutching at his arm.

'Roger, I've got to speak to you!'

He turned and saw my face. 'What is it, Sheila? Is something the matter? Have you had a message from Jack? Is it Delia?'

'No, no, nothing like that. But something terrible *has* happened and you must come at once.'

I almost dragged him away and led him out towards the kitchen courtyard, explaining in disjointed phrases what had happened, Jessie reluctantly following on behind.

When we got to the old dairy I gave him the key.

'Well done,' he said. 'That was sensible.'

The words of praise somehow made me feel better and I was able to ask, 'Do you need us to come in?'

He looked at me and said sympathetically, 'No, that won't be necessary. You stay here, out in the air. You look as if you're going to pass out.'

Jessie made as if to go in with him, saying, 'While I'm here, then, I might as well get those plates Miss Eleanor wanted.'

Roger gently barred the way.

43

'No, I'm sorry, we mustn't touch anything for the moment, and I'd be grateful, Jessie – it is Jessie? – if you would very kindly stay with Mrs Malory. I don't think she feels very well.'

Jessie looked at me as if for the first time since our horrible discovery.

'You poor soul,' she said compassionately. 'You've taken it really bad. Here, sit down for a bit.'

She led me over to an old stone mounting-block that stood in the corner of the yard and I sat down gratefully. My knees seemed to give way under me. I wondered in a detached sort of way how I would ever get up again. The lead cisterns in the courtyard were planted with stocks and their rich scent hung on the evening air, and I knew that I would never be able to enjoy that scent again because of this moment. After a while Roger came out again, locked the door behind him and said to Jessie, 'I need a telephone. I must get on to the station at Taunton. Will you show me where it is? And we must stop anyone leaving.'

'What about the rest of the concert?' I asked helplessly. 'What should we do?'

'I'd better speak to your friend Eleanor, I suppose. I don't imagine anyone will feel much like going on in the circumstances.'

'I must tell Miss Eleanor about the plates.' Jessie seemed oblivious of anything but those wretched plates, I thought, but perhaps that was her way of pushing the real horror out of her mind.

Roger helped me to my feet and we went back into the house.

We found Eleanor still supervising the buffet and Roger drew her to one side.

'Something terrible has happened,' he said quietly. I noticed almost academically that he used the same words I had, but I suppose there are not many phrases for breaking that sort of news.

'Adrian Palgrave has been murdered, in the old dairy. Jessie, here, found him and told Mrs Malory . . .'

I was staring at the poppies on Eleanor's skirt; they seemed to hypnotize me. Blood-red on black, like the red blood running down on to Adrian's black dinner jacket, red and black, they swam in front of my eyes. As if from a distance I heard Eleanor's voice say, 'Sheila, are you all right!'

The room seemed unbearably hot and I tried to pull at the high neck of my blouse to loosen it. Someone took my arm and half-led, half-carried me into another room and laid me on a sofa. I lay still for a while, trying to breathe deeply and slowly, and gradually I recovered myself and saw that Eleanor was kneeling beside me.

'I'm sorry,' I said. 'Being such a nuisance. I'm so sorry.'

She was rubbing my hand between hers.

'You're cold as ice,' she said. And it was true, I found I was shivering.

'Just a sec.' She went away and returned with a travelling rug that she put over me.

'You poor old thing,' she said, 'it's shock. You've had a rotten time. I wouldn't have had this happen for the world.'

I was grateful for her concern and compassion. Eleanor was a good person to be with at such a time, she was an old friend and I felt comfortable with her.

'You really ought to have some hot, sweet tea. Shall I get Jessie to make some?' Her large, round face was tense with anxiety.

'No, I don't think I could manage that—'

'Well, brandy then.'

She went over to a sideboard and poured some into a glass.

'This should buck you up. Drink it slowly.'

I sat up cautiously and sipped the brandy.

'What about Jessie?' I asked. 'It must have been an even greater shock for her. She found poor Adrian.'

'She's better being busy, I think,' Eleanor said. 'I tried to make her go and lie down but she said she'd rather see to the coffee for everyone. We thought that was the best thing to keep them all quiet for a bit.'

45

I made as if to get up.

'What's happening? Have the police arrived? Has everyone got to stay?'

Eleanor pushed me gently back on to the sofa.

'You stay where you are. Everything's under control. I must say your Roger's jolly efficient, he had things organized in two ticks.'

I had been obsessed with my own feelings and malaise but now I finished the brandy and felt more stable the full realization of what had happened suddenly swept over me.

'Oh, Eleanor! Adrian! He's dead. Murdered!'

The word hung in the air for a moment while we looked at each other.

'I know,' Eleanor said, 'it's terrible.'

That word again. But what I felt as I looked at Adrian's body had not been terror, more like revulsion and a kind of pity, a more intense version of the feeling I have for the poor mangled corpse of rabbit, fox, or badger at the side of the road.

'Will you have some more brandy?' Eleanor took the glass from my hand.

'No, thanks. I'm all right now.'

'No, look, you stay here for a bit. I must go and see to things – the musicians – I must get a car to take them to their hotel. But you're not to move. Stay quietly. I won't let anyone come in and bother you and I'll send Rosemary to sit with you.'

I protested that I didn't need anyone, but she was gone.

I could hear people milling about and voices outside the room and then I saw blue flashing lights outside the window and the sound of several cars on the gravel, so I knew that the police had arrived.

After a while Rosemary came in. 'How are you?' she asked anxiously. 'Roger said you'd passed out. Not surprising after what happened.'

'I'm fine,' I assured her. 'But Eleanor made me promise to sit quietly for a bit. What's happening?'

'Roger's been marvellous.' Rosemary said with pride, 'I've never seen him in action before. Very polite but very firm. Sally Stevens thought she might draw attention to herself by having hysterics and he *quelled* her with a look!'

I giggled faintly.

'What a missed opportunity for Oliver. From his expression this evening I'm sure he'd have really enjoyed slapping her face!'

'*You're* feeling better,' Rosemary said, smiling. 'Back to your old bitchy self.'

I got up slightly unsteadily from the sofa and said, 'What's going on? Are the police keeping everyone here? Are they questioning them?'

'They've taken everyone's name and address, but most of the audience can go home. Roger says he wants to talk to the members of the committee before they leave, though.'

'Enid!' I said suddenly. 'Poor soul. How is she?'

'Still pretty stunned, I think. I don't think she's really taken it in yet. Will's looking after her.'

Will always gravitated to the weak, the helpless and those in trouble. I moved towards the door.

'I must go and see if there's anything I can do to help. Poor Eleanor – such a lot to see to. She really has turned up trumps, as she would say, this evening!'

'Yes, she's very practical, a sort of Girl-Guide efficiency,' Rosemary said. 'And she's got a kind heart.'

'Well, thank God for it tonight,' I replied.

'Don't you think you ought to rest for a bit longer?' Rosemary said doubtfully. 'You still look rather pale.'

'No, I'm fine. I'd rather be doing something, like Jessie.'

I explained about Jessie's obsession with the plates.

'Poor thing,' Rosemary said. 'It must have been really horrific, switching on the light and finding him there like that!'

'I know. At least I knew there was something wrong

before I went in there. And yet, you know, it's odd; she didn't seem upset. I mean, *really* upset.'

'Perhaps it hasn't really sunk in. There's such a thing as delayed shock.'

'Yes, I suppose so. Her first reaction seemed to be that Eleanor shouldn't see – it . . .'

'Yes, well, she's devoted to Eleanor, more like a nanny, although she's so much younger.'

We went back into the Great Hall, where a couple of policemen were taking the names and addresses of the few remaining people who were leaving. Presently only the members of the committee were left, huddled together in a small group as if for mutual protection.

I looked at them one by one, curious to see how each had reacted to this dreadful happening.

Enid was at the centre of the group, with Geraldine and Evelyn on either side of her, each of them just a little excited to be even obliquely of importance. Will was leaning over Enid's chair talking earnestly to her and she, who had never really cared for Will, was looking up at him with a strange mixture of disapprobation and gratitude.

A little apart from the group, Father Freddy was standing apparently lost in thought, his long cloak wrapped around him as if for comfort, though it was quite warm in the Hall. Just for once he looked his age, an old man distressed and somehow helpless. I didn't imagine that Enid, like Adrian a positively affirmed atheist, would have accepted any comfort that he might have been able to offer.

The Stevens were sitting together at the end of a row of chairs, where I had been sitting by Sir Ernest's portrait, not speaking to each other but staring stonily ahead. They had the appearance of two people who were still in the middle of a quarrel and frustrated that they couldn't pursue it in public. She had a short fur jacket over her chiffon dress; every so often she pulled it together and gave a theatrical shudder which left Oliver unmoved. I wondered why they were still there, since neither of them was a committee member. They didn't look as if they had remained behind by choice.

I was glad to see that Eleanor was sitting down at last. Robin had just brought her a cup of coffee and she looked up at him gratefully, laying her hand lightly on his arm, and he smiled briefly. He was looking very white and strained and was obviously under some sort of pressure. I wondered what it might be – I couldn't believe that it was grief for Adrian.

Jessie came into the hall with a tray of coffee and biscuits, both of which I accepted gratefully. To my surprise I now found that I was very hungry.

'How are you, Jessie?' I asked.

'Quite all right, thank you, Mrs Malory. What about yourself? Shouldn't you still be resting? I'm sure Miss Eleanor thinks you should be.'

'No, honestly, Jessie. I'm fine. Rather ashamed of making such a fuss when you, who had the much greater shock, are so composed!' She smiled her warm Welsh smile.

'Oh, well, Mrs Malory, like Sir Ernest used to say, the Lord gives us strength to cope with the trials he sends us!'

I was amused to find that Jessie, too, had taken to quoting Sir Ernest's trite remarks. Still, if it gave her comfort at a time like this . . .

'Well,' I said, taking another biscuit, 'I think you've been marvellous.' She smiled and moved on with her tray and I nerved myself to go over to speak to Enid.

Will glanced up as I approached and looked at me critically but didn't say anything.

'Enid, my dear,' I said, 'I'm so very sorry. I simply don't know what to say . . .'

'It's been the most terrible shock to me,' she began in her high, affected voice. 'I have always been particularly sensitive to violence in any shape or form and so has Adrian.'

49

Speaking his name made her suddenly break down and she started to cry, with great gasping sobs. Will knelt and cradled her in his arms, rocking her to and fro like a child.

I stood feeling inadequate and useless. Geraldine took me to one side and said confidentially, 'Enid's coming back to stay with me for a few days. Evelyn can't have her because of her old father, but we didn't think she should be on her own.'

'That's marvellous of you,' I said. 'She really will need her friends just now.'

'That's what we thought,' Geraldine said, and there was a smugness in her voice that made me want to shake her even while I admired her kindness and generosity. Enid would not be a particularly easy guest. Rosemary and Jilly came back into the room and crossed towards me.

'They've taken our statements,' Rosemary said.

'Did Roger take them himself?' I asked curiously.

'Oh, no.' Jilly smiled at me. 'That wouldn't have been proper! It was Sergeant Collins, such a nice man. Anyway, Roger says he'll come and see you tomorrow and talk about the details of what you saw and so on . . .' Her voice trailed away.

'It's all so unreal, somehow,' Rosemary burst out, 'someone we've known for ages getting murdered and *Roger* investigating and asking the questions, like a telly play!'

Just for a moment she looked really upset. To distract her I asked, 'What are Oliver and Sally doing here?'

She glanced over to where they were still morosely sitting. 'Goodness, *doesn't* Sally look sour!' She turned back and continued, 'Oh, Adrian and Oliver had done a programme together and Roger wants Oliver to let him have the names and addresses of some of the other people Adrian was working with.'

'I see.'

I was conscious of a great weariness and said, 'If it's all right, then, I think I'll go. I feel a bit done in.'

Jilly took my arm.

'We're going to drive you back. Michael can bring you out tomorrow to collect your car. We'll go now. Roger will probably be here all night.' She glanced resignedly at where he was in earnest conversation with Sergeant Collins. 'He'll get a lift back in one of the police cars.'

'Bless you,' I replied, 'I shall be glad of a lift. And you'll want to get back to Delia.'

I listened gratefully to Jilly's chat about the baby as we drove back towards Taviscombe in the deeping dusk, the headlights of oncoming cars flashing painfully into my aching eyes.

Chapter Five

I'd finished my breakfast the next morning and was just
doing the washing up when the telephone rang. It was
Roger, to say that he would be calling to see me at about
ten o'clock. I'd managed to put the events of the previous
evening more or less out of my mind and suddenly the
horribleness of the whole thing swept over me again.
Sensing my mood, Foss began to weave around my legs
wailing loudly. I picked him up and held him close, com-
forted by the warm, furry body. He purred for a while
and then impatiently wriggled free and headed for the
kitchen, where he sat expectantly gazing at the fridge
door. I scooped some cat food out of an opened tin (I
didn't feel I could bear to cut up his usual raw liver) and
put the dish down in front of him. He sniffed at it briefly,
looked at me with scorn and incredulity and began, deliberately, to make scraping motions with his paw, before
turning and walking indignantly away.

I put the coffee on and laid out the crockery on a tray.
I found some chocolate digestive biscuits, which I knew
Roger liked, and put them on a plate, laying each one
carefully in a pattern round the edge, meticulously
moving them into place with the tip of my finger. Time
enough to think when Roger came.

When he did come he was brisk and matter of fact,
doing his job, all in the day's work. Which it was, of course.

'How are you? You look a bit better this morning!'

'Yes, I'm fine. Rather ashamed of having made such
a fuss.'

'Nothing to be ashamed of. It's a ghastly thing – most people react as you did. I must say, it's something I find very difficult to cope with myself. However often it happens, it always gets to you.'

'Poor Roger. You look dreadfully tired. I don't suppose you got much sleep?'

'Not much. A policeman's lot, as we know, is not an 'appy one.'

He finished his second biscuit and said, 'Now then. Let's get something down on paper.'

Quietly he took me through what had happened, so that I found myself able to look at the events objectively and clearly, unclouded by emotion, even finding Adrian's body.

'Yes, well, that seems quite straightforward. Thanks, Sheila. Now you're quite sure you didn't see him in the Hall before the concert began?'

'As I told you, he always sat at the back of the Hall, not with the rest of the committee members, and although I did turn round a couple of times to see who'd arrived, I didn't see Adrian.'

'Certainly no one remembers seeing him there. I haven't had the pathologist's report yet, but it looks as if he hadn't been dead all that long when you found him – though, of course, that dairy place was very cold. It was practically like having the body refrigerated! The last people who seem to have seen him were your friend Eleanor and that rather nervy young man'– he consulted his notes – 'Robin Turner. I gather that Adrian Palgrave arrived about four o'clock and he and Eleanor had to sort out the seating arrangements. Apparently there was a problem, not enough chairs or not the right sort, or something. Then he said he was going to check the car park and went out into the grounds, and that was the last they saw of him. Does that sound right to you? I would have thought he would have delegated that sort of minor task.'

'No, that was Adrian. Even if someone else had done

something perfectly well, he would always go and check it in a particularly officious way.'

'Sounds a tiresome man. Did he have many enemies?'

'I never know what you mean by *enemies*. Most people disliked him, some quite vehemently, but I can't see anyone feeling strongly enough to *murder* him.'

'Feelings are funny things. It can sometimes take quite a little thing to send a moderate feeling of dislike right over the top. Alternatively, it may be that Adrian Palgrave knew something really discreditable about someone, or had some piece of information that placed someone else in danger. That would be a motive. Otherwise we come down to the really basic ones, love or money. Tell me, were he and Enid a happily married couple?'

'Well, I can't say that that's the first description that would come to mind. It was more complex than that. She adored him and was immensely proud of being his wife. She loved being Mrs Palgrave, especially when he became quite famous.'

'And what about him?'

'Well, you've seen her; Rosemary and I rather meanly call her the Hobbit. He certainly didn't marry her for her looks, and she's quite a bit older than he is. But she's a basically tiresome woman, very full of herself and rather ponderous. The sort of person who finishes every single sentence, if you know what I mean.'

'I know just what you mean.'

'But she does have a lot of money – her father left her quite a bit of property in Manchester, I think it was – and we all assumed that was what he saw in her.'

'Do you think he had other female interests?'

'Rumour says so, though there have been no positive sightings, as it were. Everyone in Taviscombe being so beady-eyed, we imagine it must all go on in London.'

'Do you think she knew?'

'Oh yes, I'm pretty sure she must. You can see her, sometimes, looking at him when he's talking to another woman on the far side of the room, watchful, I think you might say, and aware. But I think she accepts it as the price she has to pay to go on being Mrs Palgrave.'

'But,' Roger persisted, 'would she go on accepting it? I mean, would there be something that even she couldn't bear?'

I tried to think.

'If he was actually going to leave her, I suppose, or humiliate her in some really public way. She's got a terrific ego. If her pride were really hurt, she might—' I broke off and regarded Roger sternly. 'You're not going to say that you think *Enid* might have killed Adrian! That's ridiculous.'

He smiled at my vehemence.

'Murder very often *is* a domestic matter, you know. We have to look at the obvious first.'

'Yes,' I said doubtfully, 'I suppose so. But I can't really see it being a possibility. Incidentally, if Adrian came early, what about Enid?'

'She came with those friends of hers,' he replied, 'Geraldine and Evelyn, in Evelyn's car. But then she went off to look for Adrian. She says she couldn't find him. But, you see, there were all these people milling about before the concert. They started arriving at least an hour before the thing was due to start.'

'Yes, of course,' I said, 'part of the enjoyment is wandering round the grounds before the concert. It's really more of a social event than a musical one. And it was a glorious evening. The concert started at seven o'clock, rather early, but we always like to allow at least an hour's interval for the food. The first half of the concert lasted half an hour, so I suppose Jessie and I found him about seven thirty-fiveish. If no one saw him in the Hall, where on earth was he between, say, four thirty and then?'

'I haven't been able to question everyone yet, of course, so I suppose something may turn up. A member of the audience may remember something.'

'Yes, of course. He was quite a well-known figure, after all. People would have noticed him if he'd been around the house or garden. Would you like another cup of coffee?'

'Thank you. I think I'll have it black this time, it might help me to concentrate!'

I poured the coffee and he accepted the cup gratefully and took another biscuit.

'Haven't had time for any breakfast,' he explained.

'Oh Roger, that's so bad for you, you'll get an ulcer! Let me get you a sandwich or something.'

'No, honestly, the biscuits are fine. Now then. Back to our basic motives. We've considered love, what about money?'

'Well, as I said, most of the money there was Enid's. Adrian didn't have a staff job at the BBC, he was a freelance.'

'I see. And being a poet, even a well-known one, isn't exactly lucrative.'

'No,' I replied, 'but being a biographer can be. Did you know that he's been appointed Laurence Meredith's literary executor? He's writing the official biography *and* editing the letters. I should think he's got a pretty substantial publisher's advance. They're bound to be bestsellers. Meredith was a tremendous gossip and knew practically everyone on the pre-war literary scene – really rich material there!'

'I wonder who will do it now?' Roger said meditatively.

'Goodness, how stupid of me, I'm still talking in the present tense! I just can't take in the fact that Adrian's dead, even though—'

I broke off and Roger said hastily, 'Who do you think his publishers will appoint to do them now?'

'I don't really know. There's Pritchard, of course . . . Roger, did you find a weapon?'

He hesitated for a moment and then said, 'No. Well, I'm still not sure. There were several objects in the dairy that *could* have been used to kill him, of course – an old flat-iron, a heavy metal doorstop, a copper skillet. Several things, as I say. They're all being tested for bloodstains and . . . and so forth.'

I shuddered.

'Do you think he was actually killed sitting in that chair?'

'Again, I need forensic evidence to be sure, but it looks like it.'

'So he must have known his killer. Well, if you think about it, Adrian must have felt very much at ease with whoever it was to let him stand behind his chair like that.'

'Or her.'

'You think it could have been a woman?'

'It didn't need all that amount of strength to crack him over the head with a fairly heavy object.'

'No, I suppose not.'

'Well. Thanks for the coffee and all your help. If I may I'd like to have another word when I've interviewed everyone. You know all these people – you know the undercurrents and are aware of the things they *don't* say! And, most important, you have a writer's curiosity and observation.'

'What you mean to say is that I'm dreadfully inquisitive,' I laughed. 'You're perfectly right about that.'

'I wouldn't dream of saying such a thing, but it would certainly make my job easier if you were to keep your eye on people, see if they react in character. That sort of evaluation is something you're very good at; I've always liked that in your books of criticism. I've often thought you ought to write a novel.'

'Goodness, no, I'd never be able to think of a plot.'

Roger rose to his feet. 'Well, I'll be in touch,' he said.

I went over to the sideboard and took a bar of chocolate from a dish.

'Put that in your pocket,' I said, 'in case you don't get any lunch either.'

'Now I know why Michael always looks so well fed,' he said, smiling at me.

'Well fed, or fed up? I do rather go *on* about proper meals and things.'

'It's always nice to know that people care,' he said. 'I shall be just the same about Delia!'

When Roger had gone I realized that I felt much better, as if, in talking to him, I had been able to purge my mind of the horror and retain only an intellectual interest. I suppose it wouldn't have been possible if I had actually liked Adrian, but since no emotions were involved, I would have been less than honest if I denied that I found the mystery intriguing.

I suddenly felt full of energy and went upstairs to change my bed. As I was engaged in my usual Laocoan struggle, trying to change the duvet, the telephone rang. It was Will to see how I was.

'I'm fine,' I said, 'back to normal. Ashamed of making a fuss. Think of poor Enid. I must ring her at Geraldine's'

'I rang this morning. She had a good night, I gather, but she's still very shaken (those are Geraldine's words not mine) so she's staying there for a bit. Have the police been to see you?'

'Yes, Roger's only just left.'

'Of course, I forgot, he's practically a relation, so his visit won't have left you frail and exhausted.'

'He's very thorough and highly intelligent,' I said reprovingly. 'If anyone can get to the bottom of this awful business he can.'

'Have the police got anywhere yet, do you think?'

'It's early days,' I said cautiously, not knowing how much of what Roger had told me was confidential. 'And there were so *many* people milling about before the concert, which, I suppose, is when Adrian was killed. Though, come to think of it, it could have been *during* . . .'

'Unlikely,' Will said briskly. 'Surely he was killed by someone who knew him quite well. It wasn't casual robbery, and an itinerant homicidal maniac seems unlikely. And *we* were all in the Hall listening to those lovely madrigals.'

'And all through that beautiful music Adrian was lying there, like that.'

'Stop it, Sheila!' Will said sharply. 'That's self-indulgent and you know it!'

I laughed shakily. 'Yes, Will.'

To change the subject I said, 'How is the final draft of the play?'

'Finished and with the producer. Actually, that's why I'm ringing now. I've got to go up to town and wrestle with him about one or two changes he wants me to make, and I wanted to see how you were before I went. Also – are you going to be up there yourself in the next few days? Because I rather want to see the new Bennett play and I can't think of anyone I'd rather see it with than you.'

'Oh yes, I *do* want to see that. I can certainly arrange to do a little quiet research in the British Library this week. It's very handy having Michael at home just now, I can go off at a moment's notice and not worry about leaving the animals.'

'Having left Michael enough food to see him through a long drawn-out siege, of course.'

'Of course,' I agreed. 'So, yes, please. Leave a message for me at my club about which evening. I'll really look forward to it.'

I went back to my bed-making in a more cheerful frame of mind. Then, finding Foss had got inside the duvet cover and was curled up fast asleep, I abandoned the whole project for the time being and went downstairs to make a chocolate mousse for Michael's supper.

Chapter Six

Enid phoned the next day, brisk and apparently her old self.

'I'll be staying on here with Geraldine for a little while longer,' she said. 'I feel I need the time to re-evaluate my life.'

There didn't seem to be an answer to that so I made general murmuring noises and Enid continued, 'I've been in touch with Adrian's publishers and I have arranged to take over his work on Laurence Meredith – the collected letters and the biography. I'm sure that is what Adrian would have wished and I feel I must put aside my own work until what he had started is completed.'

I was absolutely stunned by Enid's pronouncement – after all there is quite a difference between doing a major literary biography and collecting recipes (though in some cases, I must admit, one would rather read the recipes than the biography).

'Had Adrian done much work on the Meredith papers?' I asked.

'A certain amount, but of course there will be a great deal still to do.'

'There will be a lot of research . . .' I ventured.

'Certainly,' she replied sharply, 'though naturally I am used to research. When I was writing *Lampreys and Lovage* I spent many long hours in the County Archive.'

'Yes, of *course*,' I replied humbly, overwhelmed as I always was by Enid's peremptory manner.

'It is possible,' Enid continued, 'that there may be

60

certain technical matters about which I will need to consult you – that is why I am telephoning – but I am sure there will be no difficulty.'

'No,' I agreed, 'I'm sure there won't be.'

'If you were to come round here tomorrow I could put you more fully in the picture.'

'I'm sorry, Enid,' I said, 'but I'm afraid I have to go to London tomorrow.'

'Is it important? Can't you put it off? I am very anxious to get started and I need your help in drawing up a schema for the work.'

'No,' I replied firmly, 'I have several appointments that I must keep. I'll only be gone a few days. I'll ring you when I'm back.'

'Very well,' she replied grudgingly, 'I suppose that will have to do.'

After a little more conversation along these lines she rang off and I stood with the telephone receiver still in my hand fuming.

'Well, *really*!' I exclaimed to Foss, who had wandered into the room on the off chance that I might be going to open a tin of something. 'That woman!'

Foss regarded me enquiringly, wailed sympathetically, and sprang up on to the telephone table. I slammed the receiver down and he looked at me reproachfully.

'I mean,' I continued, 'I'm sorry about Adrian and all that but she really is the utter limit!'

Rosemary echoed my sentiments when I saw her in the supermarket later that day.

'You mean she had the absolute *gall* to expect you to help her write this book.'

'Not *help*, dear,' I said, 'nothing as *grand* as that! I imagine she sees me as a sort of dogsbody, permanently on call!'

'Anyway, whatever makes her think she can do a real book?' Rosemary demanded. 'She doesn't even write proper cookery books, I mean, like Elizabeth David or

Jane Grigson, with actual *writing* not just recipes. And, really, some of her recipes are a bit much. I tried the one for beef in old ale. I used one of the bottles of that special beer that Jack says is so marvellous – he wasn't at all pleased when he found out! – I followed the recipe *religiously* and it tasted like a piece of old blanket in brown gravy!'

'Was that an Elizabethan one? They really are quite disgusting, and some of the eighteenth century ones are almost as bad. I can't imagine how life went on, since if Enid's recipes are anything to go by, everyone must have suffered from terminal indigestion! No, I'm not just being bitchy, but I honestly don't think Enid's capable of writing the Laurence Meredith book and I must say I dread having anything to do with it.'

'How did she persuade Adrian's publishers to let her do it?'

'I expect she just said that she was going to, and given the awful way Adrian died and all that, I suppose it would have been a bit difficult to say no to her. Anyway, they probably think they can give it to one of their editors to tidy up. It's a pity – I couldn't stand Adrian as a person, or even as a poet, but he was a pretty good biographer and he'd have made a splendid job of it.'

'*You* ought to be writing it.'

Rosemary is a very loyal friend.

'Bless you, it's not my period, though I certainly would like to have a look at the papers. Meredith was a fascinating man and he knew absolutely *everyone* in the thirties. But, knowing Enid, I doubt if I'll be allowed a glimpse! Never mind, I'm off to London for a few days tomorrow. A bit of research in the British Library and dinner and a theatre with Will.'

Rosemary bent down and rearranged the tins of dog-food in her shopping trolley.

'I often wonder about you and Will,' she said tentatively. 'You have such a lot in common and you seem to enjoy each other's company . . .'

'And that's really it,' I said. 'Nothing more. Just good friends, as they say. Well, perhaps, just a little more – what is it the French call it? A sentimental friendship? Very fond . . . but we've each made our own lives since we've been on our own.'

'Michael won't be with you for ever,' Rosemary said, 'and you might be very lonely.'

I gave a little laugh.

'No one can be lonely with a houseful of animals, as you very well know. Anyway,' I changed the subject, 'is there anything I can get you in London?'

She was instantly diverted.

'Oh yes, if you *would* be an angel and see if you can get me that skirt in size sixteen. You know, the pleated one I got from the Taunton M & S that was too small, they hadn't got the larger size. But you might be able to get it in the Oxford Street one.'

A loaded trolley inexpertly guided by two small children clashed into mine and we moved into a more peaceful area behind a piled-up pyramid of special-offer tins of fruit salad.

'Is Enid still staying with Geraldine?' Rosemary asked.

'Yes, for a bit,' I replied. 'In spite of her business-as-usual manner, I think she's still very shaky, not surprisingly!'

'Goodness, no. Who on *earth* could have killed Adrian? I mean, he was a bit of a pain and *not* a very nice person, but to *kill* him!'

'I know. I've been going over that evening in my mind, you know, thinking about where everyone was . . .'

'You mean, you think it was one of the committee?'

'Roger seems to think so,' I said evasively.

'I suppose so – though there were so many people milling about at the concert. If Adrian had an enemy, someone in the BBC, or something,' she said vaguely, 'it would have been quite easy for them to *mingle* and then slip away afterwards.'

'In theory. But think about it, a stranger wouldn't have

known about the old dairy. It's a bit out of the way if you don't know the house. Adrian must have gone along there with the murderer or met him there by appointment. We – that's the committee – all know our way round Kinsford pretty well.'

'Yes, I see what you mean,' Rosemary said slowly, 'but it's a pretty horrifying thought.' She gave me a grin. 'Of course, it might have been Enid, panting to get her hands on a proper literary effort!'

'You mustn't say such things.' I laughed. 'Poor soul, she must be dreadfully upset.'

'Only because she's not the wife of an Important Literary Figure any more.'

'No,' I said firmly, 'I'm sure she loved him in her own way. She was very possessive. You know how fierce she always looked if she thought anyone was monopolizing him at parties and things. She was always at his elbow.'

'Well, he did stray a bit, and he had a pretty roving eye. He tried to chat up Jilly once, but fortunately she thought he was practically antedeluvian and was in shrieks of laughter when she told me about it.'

'Goodness! I never knew that!'

'I never let Jack know – he would have wanted to give him a good hiding.' She broke off suddenly.

'Well,' I said, 'perhaps that was it. Maybe he did stray on to someone else's territory, as it were, and the jealous husband . . . well, he might not have intended to kill him, things might have got out of hand.'

'I wonder who it could have been?' Rosemary said thoughtfully.

'It's only a vague possibility,' I said hastily. 'We don't really *know* anything.'

'No, I suppose not. Still . . . Goodness!' She looked at her watch. 'Look at the time and Jack said he'd be home for lunch today. Oh well, it'll have to be tuna salad again.' She reached up and took a tin from an adjacent shelf. 'Must dash. Let me know if you have any ideas about who it might have been. Oh, and have a lovely time in London with Will.'

I opened my mouth to say that I wasn't actually *going* to London with Will, but she had gone. My friend Rosemary is an incurable romantic.

As I was carefully folding my clothes and packing them in a suitcase I thought about the possibility of Adrian's having been killed by a jealous husband or lover. There didn't seem to be a suitable candidate among the committee members, most of whom were women anyway. As far as I knew. Robin didn't have any sort of girlfriend, Father Freddy was too old and, in any case, known to be celibate. And Will. Will was a widower.

'So that's no good, Tris,' I said to the small white figure who was watching my packing activities with a reproachful gaze. The dogs always come and sit looking miserable as soon as a suitcase is brought out of the cupboard on the landing, trying to make me feel guilty. Which I do. Every time. Tris made a small whining noise which I chose to interpret as encouragement.

'Hang on, though, what about Oliver? Not committee, certainly, but he knew Adrian better than most of us and he'd been to Kinsford enough times to know his way around. Yes, come to think of it, Eleanor took us all round to show us the kitchen courtyard and the outbuildings when we were doing that pageant thing that Oliver helped with. They stored the props in the old dairy. It *might* have been Oliver – I bet Sally would have given Adrian quite a bit of encouragement, since he was fairly famous. She's such a little bird-brain, she'd have been flattered if someone she thought of as intellectual fancied her. She'd have buttered him up and told him how *marvellous* he was, I'm sure. And I suppose she's still quite pretty in a way – if you like that sort of thing.'

Tris gave a loud sneeze and rubbed his nose with his paw and I gave my mind to the matter in hand and got on with my packing.

I had a lovely time in London. I did some good, solid work in the British Library, which is something I always enjoy, and my theatre trip with Will was splendid. The play was marvellous – so much so, in fact, that Will was moved to exclaim 'Oh yes! Perfect!' quite loudly at the beginning of the second act and was vigorously shushed by the people in front. We had supper at the Savoy afterwards (Will said that he'd won the battle with his producer and we ought to celebrate), something that doesn't happen to me very often.

In the taxi going to Paddington, though, I realized that I had done it again. I'm always early for everything, not just punctual, but very early indeed. It is something that I have passed on to Michael, something, he maintains, that has shortened his life.

'The time I spend waiting about, Ma,' he says, 'I could have not just read *War and Peace* – I could have *written* it!'

I am particularly early for trains and this time I realized that once again I had arrived in time to catch the train before the one I'd reserved a seat on. Naturally frugal, I didn't like to think of having wasted a booking fee, but on the other hand Paddington (which now has a new roof, but still nowhere to sit down) is not the ideal place to pass a whole hour. The train was about to depart and, making what I felt at the time was probably the wrong decision, I leapt on board.

As always the train was very crowded, more so than usual since the school holidays had just begun. As I struggled through compartment after compartment, I was jostled by waist-high figures already on their way to and from the buffet with cans of cola and hamburgers. Harassed mothers were beseeching little Debbie or little Jason to sit quietly and colour in their nice book or listen to their Walkman, and there was a continuous rustle of crisp packets and the sound of chocolate bars being unwrapped. I was forcibly reminded of Robert Benchley's remark that there are two kinds of travel: first class or with children. This decided me. Much as I begrudged the expense, I decided to travel first class and pay the extra.

I made my way through into the blissful quiet of the first-class carriages. Even these were quite full, some occupied by middle-aged businessmen deeply absorbed in the contents of their briefcases. Some (which I avoided) had younger men ostentatiously busy on portable phones. I was passing by a carriage with a single occupant, a plump man who turned, recognized me, and beckoned me in. It was Oliver Stevens. I was a little put out, because I do like to have a nice, peaceful read on railway journeys, but it would have been churlish to have ignored his signal so I smiled and slid open the carriage door. As I sat down beside him I realized with dismay that he had had rather too much to drink. He wasn't aggressively drunk, but his speech was slurred and his manner was even more expansive than usual.

'Sheila, my old love, come on in. Lovely to see you. Been up to the Smoke for a little fling? Who's the lucky chap?'

He half rose to his feet as I heaved my case up on to the rack but flopped back into his seat again like a large gasping fish.

'Hallo, Oliver,' I said, 'No, please don't bother, I can manage perfectly well.'

He gave me a vacuous smile.

'Had *rather* a good lunch. Some agency – wants me to make a telly commercial. Lots of money. Lot of crap, but lots of money.'

The ticket inspector came in and I paid him my extra fare.

Oliver was struggling to get his wallet out of his pocket.

'You should let me do that Sheila, love,' he said, 'a privilege to have the company of a charming lady . . . Lots of money . . .'

'It's very sweet of you, Oliver, but it's done now. Can I help you find your ticket?'

He held his wallet out to me like a small child asking nanny to help, and I managed to find his ticket and gave it to the inspector, who glanced at us both severely, punched the ticket and withdrew in an atmosphere of disapproval.

'He thinks I'm drunk,' Oliver said. 'That chap thinks I'm drunk.'

'Well, you're not exactly sober.' I smiled. 'It must have been a *very* good lunch!'

Oliver embarked on a circular conversation about the lunch, the agency people, television commercials, and the lovely money, which I didn't really listen to. Fond as I am of Oliver, I really can't be doing with people when they've had too much to drink. I began to wish that I'd settled for the rampaging children.

'Need lots of money for Sally,' Oliver was saying, 'for Sally's bloody horses – do you know how much a horse *eats*? – for Sally's bloody winter sports, for Sally's bloody Caribbean holidays . . .' He was now embarked on a litany of Sally's extravagances, which I (and all his friends) had heard before. I could have pointed out that his own life style (good food and wine, travel, expensive cars, the very best guns and fly rods) was equally expensive, but I knew that once Oliver was embarked on this theme he didn't even notice interruptions.

'Costs a bloody *mint*, the whole thing. Take that great house – a fortune to heat it, always needs painting, like the bloody Forth Bridge, believe me, two gardeners eating their heads off . . . Sally has to have—'

He broke off and gave me a conspiratorial glance.

'Got to keep her sweet, though. A very difficult woman, my wife. Well, you know that. Clever woman like you, you know these things. Jealous, that's what she is. Jealous as hell. Never caught me out, though! Never!'

He laughed triumphantly. 'Not for want of trying, but never caught me out.'

His mood suddenly changed.

'That bloody little bastard Palgrave, he tried to do the dirty on me. Don't like Palgrave. No,' he said forcibly, 'I don't like Palgrave. I hate the little sod. Hate! No,' he corrected himself, 'hated. He's dead now – good thing, too. Do you know what the little swine was going to do? He was going to tell Sally about Karen. There now, what do you think about that! Did you ever hear of such miserable' – he sought for another word to convey the enormity of the action and couldn't find one – 'such *miserable* behaviour. Had a little difference over that script – all his fault, stupid little bastard, a lot of bloody nonsense about social and moral values. *Moral values.*' He gave a loud snort of laughter. 'I told him, "You're the last one to be talking about moral values, chum," I said. And then we got into a silly sort of slanging match, bloody stupid, shouting at each other like kids. He got on his high horse – you know how he did – affected bastard – and said it was his duty, his *duty* mind you, to let Sally know about Karen. Said she had a right to know. Don't know how he found out. I do, though, bloody BBC gossip. Knew all about that trip to Rome and everything. Bloody gossip.'

He laid his hand on my arm and looked at me earnestly.

'I can tell you these things, Sheila, because you're a friend and you're understanding and dis— discreet. You wouldn't tell Sally about Karen? No, of course you wouldn't, you're *discreet*. And you're a bloody sensible woman. You know that a bloke's got to have a bit of *comfort* when he's married to someone like Sally. You understand, don't you, Sheila?'

He leaned even further towards me and peered up into my face.

'Course you do. Peter was a damned lucky chap. Fine woman like you. *He* didn't need any comfort . . .'

His voice trailed away and he flopped back in his seat, shifted around a couple of times and was suddenly asleep. I looked at him with distaste. His mouth had fallen open and a lock of his sparse hair hung down over his round face, that was now red and glistening with sweat. I wondered how Karen – she sounded quite young – could bear to look at that face first thing in the morning. Since Oliver showed a distressing tendency to lean towards me and rest his head on my shoulder. I moved to the other side of the compartment, opened my book, and tried to ignore the snorting noises that came from his recumbent figure.

As the train was running through the Somerset Levels, nearing Taunton, I got up and shook his shoulder.

'Oliver, wake up, we're almost there!'

He opened his eyes and looked at me blearily.

'Sheila? What's the matter?'

'We're almost at Taunton,' I said. 'You've been asleep.'

He tried to pull himself together and put his hand to his head.

'God! I feel awful!'

'I think you had rather a lot to drink,' I said.

'God, yes, that lunch! Can't remember all that much after they put me in a taxi! Hope I didn't make a nuisance of myself . . .'

'No,' I said, 'you talked a bit and then you fell asleep.'

'Thank God for that. Sorry, Sheila, old love. I've had a bit of a week, actually . . .'

The train drew into the station and I said, 'How are you going to get home from Taunton? Is Sally meeting you?'

'No, I'll get a taxi.'

'I'll run you back,' I said. 'I left my car at the station.'

'That's good of you, Sheila. But do you mind if we just slip into the buffet so that I can get a cup of coffee and take an aspirin? What was it Dorothy Parker said about her head feeling like something left over from the French Revolution?'

The coffee seemed to do him good and on the drive home he was more or less his old self. I wasn't sure if he had any memory at all of what he had told me, so I kept up a flow of innocuous chatter about the play I'd seen and the theatre in general and, refusing an invitation to go in for a drink, dropped him off at the bottom of his drive.

70

I arrived home just after Michael.

'Hello, love, is that a kettle just by your hand? Bless you, I really do *need* a cup of tea. I've had the most *exhausting* couple of hours!'

I told him, in graphic detail, about my journey from Paddington.

'What extraordinary things seem to happen to you, Ma,' Michael said, pouring out a cup of tea and pushing it towards me.

'It was a maddening waste of a first-class ticket,' I said resentfully, 'having to listen to Oliver going on like that.'

Michael ripped open a new packet of Bourbons and bit into one thoughtfully.

'Of course, if Adrian Palgrave *was* going to tell the dreaded Sally that Oliver was playing away from home, and if she *was* going to take it very hard, like divorce, even, then I suppose your friend Oliver had a motive for murdering him.'

'Oh, surely not,' I said. 'I mean, I think Oliver would be quite glad to be rid of Sally – she really is an absolute pain. And then he could settle down with little Karen, or whoever.'

'Aren't you the dear old naïve thing, and after having been married to a solicitor for all those years! If there was a divorce, Sally could take him to the cleaners – half the sale price of that big house, the horses, cars, and whatnot. I know Oliver earns a pretty good whack but I don't think he could manage to support that extravagant life style on what he'd have left when she'd got at him. We've got a client at the moment who's in just that position, poor devil.'

I smiled to myself at the proprietorial 'we' and said, 'Yes, of course, how silly of me. Well, I suppose it does give him a motive. But' – I thought of the fat, foolish face relaxed in sleep – 'not *Oliver*. He *couldn't* have!'

'Well, somebody did,' Michael pointed out. 'Are any of the others more likely murderer material.'

I considered the matter.

71

'Oh dear, how would one *know*? There's Robin, I suppose. He's a bit unbalanced and Adrian was pretty beastly to him. I suppose he *might* . . .'

I broke off and went to the sink to rinse out my cup.

'No, I'm *not* going to start speculating. Let Roger sort it out. It's his business, after all. Now then, what can we have for supper that I can cook in half an hour?'

Chapter Seven

I woke up the next morning feeling rather depressed. It was a gloomy day, heavy, overcast, and definitely chilly. In the kitchen I found Foss sitting with ostentatious pathos in front of the unlit Aga. He gave a faint wail, to indicate that he was barely surviving in such Arctic conditions, and I dutifully switched on the electric fire. He stretched luxuriantly in front of it and was immediately joined by the two dogs, who jostled for position behind him. I resisted an impulse to crouch down on the floor beside them and got on with the breakfast.

After the excitement of my little jaunt to London I felt disinclined to settle to the various household tasks that awaited me, including, I noticed as I slid the pan with Michael's bacon under the grill, cleaning the cooker.

After Michael had gone I stuffed clothes into the machine, secure in the knowledge that I could now say to myself that I had Done the Washing (this is a form of conscience-salving every woman is familiar with) and could now go out and potter round the shops.

When I stopped at the garage to fill up, my wretched petrol-locking cap stuck, as it often does, and I wrestled with it feeling stupid and embarrassed as people at the other pumps looked scornfully on. There was a roar and an enormous motorbike, black and menacing with a low-slung seat and great tall handle-bars, pulled up behind me and a large, heavily built figure, wearing black leathers and a spaceman's helmet, got off.

He removed the helmet, revealing a touchingly youthful face.

'Having trouble, love?' he asked.

'Yes, the tiresome thing seems to be stuck. I can't turn it.'

'Here, let me.'

He leaned over and gave it a quick twist.

'There you go.'

'Thank you *very* much, that was kind of you.'

I looked at the motor bike.

'That really is a splendid machine. A Harley-Davidson, isn't it? My son always longed for one, but they cost the earth!'

His face lit up.

'Yeah – she's brilliant! A 1000cc sportster. Post-'82. Fabulous torque – you can go from forty to one hundred and ten without changing gear. And stable! You can take a tight corner and grind all the chrome off the pegs!'

We smiled at each other in pure pleasure at such a paragon and his delight in her and I went on my way inexplicably cheered by the encounter.

Half-way down Fore Street I caught sight of Enid on the other side of the road and, rather meanly, dived into Boots to avoid her. I really didn't feel that I could face a long session about the Meredith book and hoped she would think that I was still in London. To kill time until I felt it was safe to go outside again I wandered round, trying out the new perfumes and idly wondering if a brightening rinse to bring out the highlights would produce a newer, better Me. As I rounded the Baby Care shelves I ran into Rosemary anxiously surveying the jars of baby food.

'They don't seem to have any of that strained pear left,' she said. 'Actually, Delia's really eating ordinary things now, but she still loves that squashed-up pear.'

'Are they still with you?' I asked.

'Jilly and Delia are, yes,' she said. 'And Roger's back and forth between here and Taunton. It's lovely to have them, but of course Mother's carrying on about my not spending so much time with her. You can't win! I really feel like a wrung-out rag sometimes!'

'Come and have a cup of coffee,' I said. 'You'll feel much better after a nice sit-down.'

'I shouldn't really,' Rosemary said, 'but what the hell.'

I paused in the doorway of Boots and scanned the street cautiously but Enid was nowhere in sight. Nor, thank goodness, was she lurking in the recesses of the Buttery. Rosemary and I sat with our coffee and comforting doughnuts both feeling definitely cheered.

'Small, simple pleasures,' Rosemary said. 'It doesn't take much to make us feel better!'

'Women are luckier than men,' I agreed. '*They* seem to need *much* more!'

'Yes, they are gloomier on the whole.' Rosemary considered the problem. 'All the troubles of the world on their shoulders?'

'Poor things!' I said and we both laughed.

'Mind you,' Rosemary suddenly looked serious. 'Something rather upsetting *has* happened and Jack's very worried about it.'

'What's happened?'

'Robin's gone off somewhere without saying anything to anyone, and no one seems to know where he is.'

'Good heavens, how extraordinary!'

'He didn't come in to work at all this week so Jack sent someone round to his flat.'

Robin worked for Jack's firm, which is why Rosemary has always taken an interest in him.

'And he wasn't there?'

'Not a sign of him, and the papers cancelled at short notice. I asked at the newsagent.'

'Oh dear.'

'Yes, well, we couldn't help wondering. He *did* get terribly upset that night – he was talking quite wildly after the committee meeting, all about how Adrian was out to get him and how he hated him. I didn't take a lot of notice at the time, well, I just thought he was a bit agitated. But you know he did have that break-down not so long ago.'

'But surely Robin wasn't *violent*,' I said.

'No,' she agreed, 'but you never know how these things

are going to take people. Robin was quite obsessive about Adrian. It was almost a persecution complex.'

'Oh dear,' I said again.

Rosemary fished in her bag and produced a tissue to wipe her jammy fingers.

'Actually,' she said slowly, 'Jack did have to tell Roger. We felt rather awful about it, but Jack thought he ought to know.'

'Yes, of course, you had no choice. And Roger's so very understanding. I mean he wouldn't immediately assume that Robin was the murderer . . .'

'Oh, Sheila, he *couldn't* be, surely not. Not *Robin*!'

'Well, I wouldn't have thought so, but as we said, you never know how people like that are going to react.'

'If it *was* Robin, who, you know, killed Adrian – and I don't for a moment think it is,' Rosemary added hastily. 'But *if* it was, then poor Eleanor is going to be very upset. It really looks as if she's taken him under her wing and it would have been so splendid for both of them.'

'That's just what I was thinking that night, the night of the concert. He was very much "son of the house", I thought.'

'Yes. Oh dear,' Rosemary sighed, 'I *do* hope everything's all right.'

'The awful thing is,' I said, 'that one likes Robin much more than one liked Adrian.'

'Have you seen anything of Eleanor, since the concert?' Rosemary asked.

'No, I keep meaning to phone, but I've been away, of course, and the time just seems to *whizz* by.'

'Don't I know it! *Where* has this year gone?' she demanded fiercely. 'We'll soon be into the hell of Christmas shopping! And Mother's being particularly demanding. As I said, she resents any time I spend with Jilly and Delia. Which reminds me, I *must* go and take her fish for lunch or my name will be mud.'

'I'll pop round and see her one afternoon,' I said. 'I feel a bit guilty. I haven't been to see her for ages.'

'You see!' Rosemary said triumphantly. 'She does it to you as well and you aren't even related to her! Still,' she continued, 'it would be nice if you could spare the time. I never thought I'd feel sorry for her, but so many of her friends – well, contemporaries, she doesn't actually have *friends* – have died, and she does miss talking about the old days. There aren't many people left now who remember.'

'Yes, of course I'll go. And I'll phone first.'

Mrs Dudley's acerbic attitude to people who 'dropped in' was well known.

'Bless you.'

'And do let me know if you have any news of Robin. I'll ring Eleanor – perhaps she may know something.'

Later that afternoon Roger telephoned.

'Just to say that the inquest will be next week. I thought I'd better warn you, just in case you have to give evidence about finding the body. But we'll be asking for an adjournment so I don't expect it's very likely. How are you feeling? Quite recovered, I hope.'

'Oh yes, fine. Still rather embarrassed at nearly passing out like that, but it was the smell of the blood that did it. I never could bear it.'

There was a short silence at the other end of the line, then Roger said slowly, 'Did you say the smell of the blood?'

'Yes.'

'You could actually smell it?'

'Yes. Why, what's the matter?'

'It's just that if the blood was so fresh that you could smell it, then the murder must have taken place no more than an hour before you found him.'

'I see.'

'We've had the pathology report, of course, but they couldn't be exact about the time of death because it was so cold in there. And by the time I went in the smell had gone . . .'

77

I tried to think.

'Well,' I said, 'the first half of the concert lasted about half an hour, so Adrian must have been killed either *during* the concert or in that last half-hour . . .'

'When everyone was milling about. It's a period when it's very difficult to pin down where people were,' Roger said.

'Yes, let me think,' I said, trying to remember. 'I certainly didn't see Adrian in the Hall and Enid came in with Geraldine and Evelyn, then, a bit later, Father Freddy, then Oliver. Sally was already there. Oh yes, and then Will.'

'What about Robin?'

'Ah yes, Robin. Rosemary told me that he's gone off somewhere. Surely you don't think . . .'

'Keeping an open mind, as they say. When did he come into the Hall?'

'Oh, he was with Eleanor,' I said, 'greeting people and generally chatting.'

'Did you see him all the time until the concert started?'

'Well, no, I suppose, not *all* the time. There were so many people there and a lot of coming and going. Well, you saw for yourself what it was like. Eleanor will be able to tell you, though.'

'Yes, I'll have a word.'

There was another pause.

'Sheila, I don't like to ask you this – they're all friends of yours – but you would tell me, wouldn't you, if you remembered anything, or if anyone said anything?'

I thought of my train journey from Paddington.

'Oh dear,' I said reluctantly. 'Yes, well, there *is* something. It might not be anything at all, but I suppose you'd better know.'

And I told him what Oliver had said about Adrian's threat to tell Sally about his affair.

'And I think Sally *might* divorce him, if she thought she could really get her hands on most of the money and property.'

'Leaving him practically nothing?'

'And it wouldn't surprise me if they had put a lot of stuff in Sally's name to save tax. Oliver's the sort of man who would have a good accountant.'

'Well, that's very interesting.'

'Roger,' I said, 'if you do delve into all that – well, I don't think Oliver remembers much of that conversation we had, but still . . . I do feel rather awful telling you about it.'

'Yes, I know.' His voice softened. 'I'm sorry, Sheila. I don't want you to feel like some sort of informer, but we really do need all the help we can get to catch Palgrave's killer. It was a thoroughly brutal crime – well, I don't need to tell you that – and there's no guarantee that the murderer won't strike again. But of course I won't give any sort of hint about where I heard anything. Your friend Oliver knew that I was going to make a few enquiries around the BBC about Palgrave, so he'll assume I got it from there.'

But I did feel badly about it. I put down the phone and went to make a cup of tea. In the kitchen both dogs were asleep in their baskets and Foss was sitting on the worktop staring morosely out at the fine rain that was falling. As I plugged in the kettle he jumped down and went to the back door demanding to be let out. We both stood in the doorway watching the low cloud rolling down from the hills above the house. Then he gave me a reproachful look and stalked back into the house, and I heard his resentful wails as he marched upstairs to his wet-weather lair in the airing cupboard. I poured myself a cup of tea and reached for the biscuit tin. It was, I told myself, a perfectly reasonable occasion for comfort eating.

A few days later I had to go to my doctor. I have tiresome ears that go deaf on me every few months and have to be syringed. The receptionist said (as she always did), 'He's running a bit late today,' and I went into the waiting-room not sorry to have a quiet sit-down, flicking through the rather elderly magazines. There was one other person before me, Jessie Thomas. She was sitting with a magazine open on her lap, but obviously not reading it.

'Hello, Jessie,' I said in some surprise. Jessie was never ill. 'What's the matter?'

She looked up, startled at being addressed.

'Oh, Mrs Malory, you did give me a turn. I was miles away.'

'Are you not well?' I asked.

'Oh, it's nothing, just a bit of indigestion. But Miss Eleanor she does fuss so. She made me come and see Dr Macdonald. A lot of nonsense, and so I told her. A spoonful of bicarb and I'd be fine.'

'It's not a good idea to neglect things,' I said reprovingly, 'you never know how they might develop. How long have you had it?'

'Oh, not long, it's really nothing to bother about! No need to go wasting the doctor's time.' She spoke irritably and I thought that perhaps she resented Eleanor's bossiness in packing her off to see the doctor for something that she, Jessie, considered unimportant.

To change the subject I said, 'How is Eleanor? I've been meaning to telephone to see how she is after that awful evening.'

'We had the police round the place for ages,' Jessie said, 'searching the grounds. I don't know what for, I'm sure.'

'I suppose they still haven't found the weapon. Did they say anything?'

She compressed her lips.

'I don't have anything to do with them, Mrs Malory. Young policemen, hardly more than boys, coming into my kitchen without asking. Did you ever hear the like?'

I pitied any young constable who had had the rough edge of Jessie's tongue.

'That inspector, your friend,' Jessie said accusingly. 'He was round to see Miss Eleanor yesterday. Wanting to know about poor Mr Robin.'

So he was now Mr Robin to Jessie – very much 'son of the house'.

'It was very strange,' I said, 'the way he went off like that.'

Jessie looked at me reprovingly. 'He had his own reasons, no doubt. It could have been any number of things. No need to go casting aspersions on the poor young man.'

'What did they want to know?' I asked.

'Oh, if he was with Miss Eleanor before the concert,' Jessie said, 'things like that.'

'Was he?'

'With Miss Eleanor? Yes, he was. He came nice and early in the afternoon to give her a hand, took the day off work specially. He's very thoughtful like that.'

'Was Robin there when Mr Palgrave came at four o'clock?'

'Indeed he was. Naturally he didn't want to see Mr Palgrave, not after that nasty upset they had, so he came into my kitchen and had a cup of tea and one of my cheese scones and helped me open the bottles of wine until Miss Eleanor came and fetched him again.'

'And they were together all the rest of the time?' I persisted.

'Oh, yes. Right up until nearly half an hour before the concert started and Miss Eleanor came to see me about the refreshments. We were a bit worried that the quiches hadn't arrived. That Mrs Wansford, she would insist on making four or five and she was dreadfully late bringing them. I said to Miss Eleanor, "You should've let me do the whole thing like I wanted to, then we'd have known where we are." But you know Miss Eleanor, she does hate upsetting anyone and Mrs Wansford went on so about these quiches. Did you have any of them, Mrs Malory? They didn't look up to much to me. That wholemeal pastry, you can never get it really nice and short.'

The receptionist came in and bore Jessie away before I could ask anything else. But as I sat in Dr Macdonald's surgery, holding the little enamel dish on my shoulder while the water fizzed uncomfortably round in my ear, I thought about Robin, unaccounted for in that last half-hour before the concert began. There would have been time – just – for him to have led Adrian away from the crowd, ostensibly to have a word about something, quietly, in the old dairy. Perhaps that's why Adrian was sitting down. He would have never imagined he could be in any sort of danger from Robin. I imagined him, leaning back confidently in the chair, being his patronizing and arrogant self, so that it would have been easy for Robin to approach from behind and bring the weapon (whatever it was) down with full force upon Adrian's head. I shuddered and some of the water in the enamel dish spilt over my hand.

'There you are.' Dr Macdonald handed me a tissue to dry my ear. 'Now you'll be able to hear the least little whisper.'

I mopped dutifully away. But there are some things, I thought, that one would rather not hear.

Chapter Eight

I decided to propose myself for coffee with Mrs Dudley rather than tea; she had her lunch early so I wouldn't have to stay too long. Besides, if I went to tea, most likely poor Rosemary would find herself scouring Taviscombe for some particular delicacy that her mother would declare essential for any properly constituted tea-table.

Elsie, Mrs Dudley's faithful slave, let me in.

'Mrs Malory, it's so nice to see you, you're quite a stranger!'

'I know, Elsie, but the days seem to fly by. How's that little dog of yours?'

She beamed at me with delight.

'Oh, Benjy, he's much better now. He had this nasty patch on his fur. Mr Hawkins said it was a sort of eczema, but he gave Benjy this injection. Ever so good he was, and now you can hardly see where it's been . . .'

A querulous voice from the sitting room demanded, 'Is that you, Sheila? Come in and sit down. Elsie! Stop chattering and bring in the coffee.'

Elsie and I exchanged glances and I went in to greet Mrs Dudley.

Even in the month since I had seen her last she had become more frail and mysteriously smaller as old people do. Her eyes, however, were as sharp as ever and her manner no less imperious. I had brought her some sweetpeas from my garden, since I knew she was fond of them. Her face softened at the sight of the delicate mauve, pink, and purple flowers and she touched them gently with the tip of her finger.

'Thank you, Sheila, that was very thoughtful of you. That fool Greaves sowed them too late this year and they came to nothing. I cannot imagine why I continue to employ him, he is getting very forgetful and his work is by no means what it was. The broad beans this summer have been very poor.'

Like all of Mrs Dudley's household, Greaves must be well over seventy, and it is always a source of wonder to me that he still manages to cope with her large garden.

'The garden always looks very nice,' I said placatingly as Elsie came into the room with the tray of coffee things.

'That will do, Elsie, Mrs Malory will pour,' Mrs Dudley said dismissively.

Rather nervously I lifted the heavy silver pot. It was Victorian and very ornate. I managed to pour the coffee without spilling any in the saucers and said, 'I do believe you are the only person I know who still *uses* their silver. Most people have either sold it or put it away in the bank for safety.'

Mrs Dudley dilated her nostrils contemptuously.

'I would consider it a really wicked state of affairs if I couldn't use my dear mother's silver in my own home. What is the world coming to! I was saying to that young man of Jilly's only the other day, what is the world coming to when the police cannot protect us, even in our own homes. Before the war and quite a bit after it, for that matter, I could leave my front door open all day, but now – all these bolts and bars and chains! Nowhere and nothing is safe! Look at the murder the other day. At *Kinsford* of all places. Sir Ernest must be turning in his grave!'

'I know,' I said, helping myself to a piece of Elsie's shortbread, 'it was really dreadfully upsetting.'

'There never used to be crimes of that sort in Taviscombe. At least, not among people of one's own class. Of course,' she continued, 'that man Palgrave *was* from London and goodness knows what sort of people he knew there.'

'He and Enid have lived here for quite a while,' I said. 'Ten years at least.'

84

Mrs Dudley smiled at me pityingly.

'Yes, Sheila dear, but he wasn't born here. We know nothing at all about his background. He could have been *anybody*! And I never cared for that wife of his – very opinionated!'

I remembered an occasion when Enid and Mrs Dudley had come up against one another at the Taviscombe Women's Institute some years ago, when Mrs Dudley was President and a newly arrived Enid Palgrave had dared to criticize some of the arrangements for the annual outing to the Bath and West Show.

'I believe *he* was something to do with television,' Mrs Dudley said. 'Of course I very rarely watch it myself. The news, perhaps, though that is so depressing nowadays, and the occasional church service – I can't get to St James now, all those steps! – though they do seem to have a great many services from Nonconformist or even *Catholic* churches.'

Rosemary had told me that her mother had taken to watching the racing on television in the afternoons, something that we both found quite extraordinary until Rosemary decided that Mrs Dudley had so identified with the Queen Mother that she probably felt it her *duty* to follow the sport of kings.

'Pour yourself some more coffee,' Mrs Dudley ordered, and although I didn't really want another cup I found myself lifting the heavy silver pot again. Mrs Dudley looked at me critically.

'You are looking very washed out,' she said. 'It's all this gadding about in London.'

I protested that I enjoyed going to London and that I found it very stimulating.

'I hear you went with Will Maxwell,' she said, giving me a piercing stare. I wondered how she knew that. Rosemary, I was sure, wouldn't have told her. But then Mrs Dudley's sources of information were many and various. She would have made an excellent spy-master.

'I didn't *go* to London with Will,' I said defensively, feeling that I was once again at school and up before my headmistress for some unspeakable transgression. 'I was up there to do some work in the British Library, but I did go to the theatre with him.'

'You know,' she continued, as if I had not spoken, 'and *I* know that dear Will is a perfect gentleman – his mother's brother was Sir James Hale – and he would never behave other than honourably. But it is always *unwise*, Sheila, to give people occasion for gossip.'

The effrontery of this (on several counts) rendered me speechless and I took a gulp of my now lukewarm coffee.

'Will is a dear man, but men do not always think of these things.'

It is a truly remarkable tribute to Will's sweet and generous nature that even Mrs Dudley can find nothing to criticize in him. Indeed he is one of her favourites and, as such, can do no wrong.

'Will is very kind,' I said colourlessly, hoping to change the subject.

'Too kind, sometimes,' Mrs Dudley leaned forward confidentially. 'Look at that wife of his.'

'Lucy?'

'Yes, you remember her?'

I did indeed remember Lucy Maxwell, it would be impossible to forget beauty like hers. Peter always said that she looked like everyone's idea of a fairy princess, with delicate features and a fall of straight silver blonde hair. She was a shy girl and very serious. I wondered, sometimes, if she had any sort of sense of humour and what she made of Will's plays. He met her when he was down here filming – her father, Dr Bryan, was one of our local GPs – and it was certainly love at first sight, for him at least. Will was in his forties, then, and still unmarried. She was twenty years younger and swept away by what must have seemed a very glamorous lifestyle. They were married almost immediately and lived in London and we only heard snippets of news about them from Lucy's parents, but it seemed that they were very happy. Then, after they had been married about seven years. Lucy was killed in a car accident. I never knew the details, Will never referred to it and neither did I. After Lucy's death he came down to Taviscombe to see her parents and, while he was here he bought (on an impulse, it seems) the cottage he now lives in, deep in the heart of the moor.

We have known him from those early days because Peter did some legal work for him and they liked each other and became friends. Gradually, as the years went by, Will has been drawn more and more into Taviscombe life and now he devotes quite a bit of his time to local causes and is generally considered to be a helpful and genial presence in our local society. But one is always aware of the deep melancholy that lies just below the surface cheerfulness, an emptiness that now probably never will be filled.

'Poor Will,' Mrs Dudley said, 'he was always a fool about that girl.'

'They were very much in love,' I replied.

'*He* was, certainly, absolutely besotted by her. Forgave her everything.'

'Forgave her?' I was startled and uneasy, I didn't think I wanted to hear what I knew Mrs Dudley was determined to tell me.

'Oh yes. Perfectly terrible it was. Poor Mrs Bryan was dreadfully upset when she heard about it.' Mrs Dudley's eyes were bright with malice.

'But when *was* this?' I asked.

'When she had the accident, of course, it all came out then.' She paused to consider the effect the story was having on me. Then she continued.

'It just so happened that I was having tea with Mrs Bryan that very day (she was quite a friend of mine, you know) when Will telephoned to tell her what had happened. He was quite distraught, she said, and she, poor soul, could hardly take in what had happened.'

I felt a pang of horror and a deep pity for what Will must have suffered – so much more than we had realized.

'It seems that Lucy had fallen in love with this other

man, younger than Will, of course. I always said that age difference was too great. She was quite open about it, told Will all about it. He begged her to stay but she said she was going away with this man, couldn't live without him and all that sort of rubbish.'

Mrs Dudley paused as if for some interjection, but I couldn't say anything so after a moment she went on.

'But life caught up with that young lady. The mills of God grind slowly, Sheila, I've always said so. This man took fright, had no intention of leaving his wife (she had all the money, you see), told Lucy he didn't want to see her again. Well, she was in a dreadful state, Mrs Bryan said – Will told her all this later, you understand – quite hysterical. She said she was going to see him and rushed out and got into her car and drove off like a mad thing.'

'And that,' I said slowly, 'was when she had the accident.'

'Drove straight into that lorry,' Mrs Dudley said with grim satisfaction. 'Killed outright.'

There was a moment of silence and I suddenly caught the evocative and poignant scent of the sweet-peas.

'Who was this man?' I asked.

'We never knew.' Mrs Dudley spoke with some dissatisfaction, unwilling to admit that even her intelligence network had been unable to uncover this important fact. 'But we do know that it was someone in Taviscombe. Apparently she used to meet him when she was down here seeing her parents. Naturally he had to lie low when she was killed like that – he must have known it was his fault.'

'And Lucy never told Will who it was?'

'No. And do you know, Sheila, after she died, I don't think he *wanted* to find out. It would have been too much for him, poor man.'

I was surprised at this unexpectedly sensitive remark. It was true, I am sure, that Will had closed away that part of his life for ever, or had tried to.

Elsie came into the room to take away the coffee things and I seized the opportunity to gather up my handbag and make a move to go. Unusually for her, Mrs Dudley did not try to make me stay longer and I saw that the effort of a sustained conversation tired her now. Moved, I bent down and embraced her, something I didn't normally do when I left. She looked surprised, but caught my hand and held it for a moment.

'Goodbye, Sheila. Come and see me again soon. There aren't many left, now, who remember . . .'

As I drove home my mind was full of the tragedy I had just heard. I hardly knew how I could face Will again, knowing what I did. His kindness and gentle humour seemed almost unbearably sad.

That night I couldn't sleep. Something was stirring just below the surface of my mind and, as I lay tossing restlessly, I suddenly realized what it was.

Suppose Adrian had been the man that Lucy had fallen so disastrously in love with. The facts fitted. Adrian was rumoured to have had several affairs, but, as everyone knew, he wouldn't leave Enid because he needed her money. Perhaps Will had found out quite recently. All those years of grieving might have built up a great wave of hatred, when nothing would suffice but the death of Lucy's betrayer. The cause of her death. Another thing struck me – Will had come in late to the concert. I pushed the thought away. It was too unbearable even to contemplate. Will couldn't kill a fly. And yet I remembered his passionate devotion to Lucy and the quiet intensity of his grief when she died. The words of the madrigal echoed through my head:

> 'My thoughts hold mortal strife,
> I do detest my life . . .'

I remembered Will sitting beside me weeping. My mind was in a whirl of misery and confusion. After a while I got up and took one of the sleeping tablets I hadn't used since the days just after Peter died, and after a while I fell into a troubled sleep.

Chapter Nine

I felt awful the next morning. I was still half dopey with the effect of the sleeping tablet. As I dragged myself around the kitchen getting Michael's breakfast and opening tins for the animals, I resolutely tried to put out of my mind the disturbing thoughts that had spoiled my rest. After all, it was pure conjecture. Indeed, it would surely have been too much of a coincidence if *Adrian* had been Lucy's lover.

'What's up, Ma?' Michael asked. 'You look like death!'

'Oh, nothing. I had a bad night, that's all.'

He looked at me quizzically but said nothing, swirling honey onto his toast in patterns in such a way that trails of it fell on to the tablecloth.

'Oh Michael, really!' I snapped. 'How can you be so childish and clumsy. Now that cloth will have to be washed and it was clean on yesterday!'

'Sorry, Ma. Stupid of me.'

He finished his toast and coffee and got up to go. As he passed my chair he put his arm around my shoulders and gave me a hug.

'Cheer up! Whatever it is, it's not the end of the world.'

I felt rather ashamed of my bad temper, but when the post arrived I found that I had cause for more irritation. There, lying on the table before me, its red lettering somehow a personal insult, was a final demand for the electricity bill.

I always pay my bills by standing order, so obviously the bank had made a stupid muddle. It suddenly seemed the last straw and I snatched up my bag, thrust my arms into my coat and drove straight into Taviscombe to give them a piece of my mind.

It didn't improve my temper when I discovered that, since the bank had only just opened, there were long queues. I tried to choose the shortest one but found myself (as I always do) first behind a shopkeeper paying in large sums in endless coins, and then someone who was engaged in a complicated foreign exchange transaction which involved much plying of calculators. Eventually the counter clerk went away entirely and showed no signs of coming back.

'Has she disappeared completely?' A voice that sounded as irritable as I felt revealed itself as Enid Palgrave.

'So you're back, then,' she continued. 'I have been trying to get in touch with you about the Meredith papers.'

'Well,' I said, trapped in the queue and unable to wriggle out of the situation. 'I am rather busy at the moment.'

She ignored my feeble reply and went on.

'There is a great deal to be done in the way of sorting and classifying. From what I have managed to read through already, the papers seem to fall into two periods. One, when he was in Paris in the nineteen-twenties and the other, Antibes in the thirties. Adrian had classified some of them . . .'

She went droning on and I listened with half an ear. The clerk had now reappeared but she had produced a sheaf of papers for the customer to sign. By now I was practically quivering with frustration and impatience. Enid's voice went relentlessly on as I half turned towards her.

'Fascinating insights . . . literary importance . . . strange coincidences . . . some very deplorable happenings . . . people of such eminence . . .'

The man in front of me was now slowly gathering up all his papers and I turned back towards the counter. Of course the clerk was apologetic, and of course it was all the fault of the computer. There was nothing that I could say I turned away, feeling cheated of a really good outburst.

'I will come and see you tomorrow,' Enid said to me as she took her place at the counter. 'In the afternoon – I'm not quite sure what time.'

It was with bad grace that I waited for Enid's visit the next day. I certainly didn't want to get involved in helping her edit the Meredith papers, but she seemed to have backed me into a corner so that, apart from a downright refusal, there wasn't much that I could do. If it had been anyone else but Enid I might have found the task enjoyable. Laurence Meredith was a brilliant and witty writer and had known many famous people. His papers would be fascinating to read. But the thought of plodding stolidly through them with Enid robbed them of much of their appeal. And, as I have already said, I really can't be doing with her as a person.

As the afternoon wore on so my resentment increased. I hate waiting for people, especially when I don't know exactly when to expect them. It's bad enough when you're waiting for the television repairman or someone you actually *want* to come! I was restless and couldn't settle to anything. At half-past four I got the dogs' leads and took them out for a walk, slamming the front door defiantly behind me. If Enid came now she could jolly well go away again.

When I returned and there was still no sign of her having called, I decided to ring up Geraldine. She answered the phone almost at the first ring and spoke in a fast agitated voice.

'Hello – is that the police?'

'Geraldine, whatever's happened? It's Sheila, Sheila Malory.'

There was a slight pause while Geraldine appeared to collect herself. Then she said, 'Oh, Sheila, it's you. What do you want?'

'I wondered if I could have a word with Enid.'

There was another pause, then Geraldine spoke very fast.

'There's been a dreadful accident. Enid went back to the Old Schoolhouse yesterday. She was working on those papers, you know the ones I mean, and she got quite involved with them and decided not to come back here but stay the night there . . .'

Her voice tailed away and I prompted her.

'So what happened?'

'Oh, Sheila, it was awful. There was a fire – I don't think they know what caused it yet – and she's dead.'

'Oh no!'

Geraldine spoke more composedly.

'You know that she takes sleeping pills, she always has, she is a martyr to insomnia. So she didn't smell the smoke or hear the fire. The people down the lane saw the flames and called the fire brigade, but it was too late.'

'Did the house burn down entirely?' I asked.

'No, it was mostly downstairs, in Adrian's study. No, poor Enid, it was the smoke that killed her.'

Somehow it made it just a little less awful. I couldn't bear to think of Enid perishing in a flaming inferno.

'Oh, Geraldine, I'm so sorry. It's a ghastly thing to have happened.'

'If *only* she hadn't stayed there. I keep thinking that. If she'd been here, she'd still be alive. I ought to have persuaded her to come back.'

'You mustn't blame yourself,' I said soothingly. 'When Enid made up her mind to do something she was very difficult to persuade.'

'Yes, I suppose so,' Geraldine said doubtfully.

'She was supposed to have been coming to see me this afternoon,' I said. 'When she didn't turn up I wondered what had happened.'

'Oh, she was wonderful like that,' Geraldine said. 'She was never late for an appointment.'

'What was that about the police?' I asked.

'Oh, you know. There'll have to be a post-mortem, all

that sort of thing. There aren't any relations – well, I think Adrian had a cousin in New Zealand – so I feel I must do what I can. The funeral and everything.'

'That's very splendid of you, Geraldine,' I said. 'It's a thankless task.'

'It's the least I can do for Enid. Well, for Adrian, too. It will have to be a joint funeral. The police haven't released *his* body yet. It will make all the arrangements very difficult.'

Already, I noticed, the pangs of grief were being slightly mitigated by a sense of importance, of running the show as Enid herself had done. 'Well,' I said, 'if there's anything at all I can do to help, please let me know.'

'Oh, I think everything's under control.' The voice was Geraldine's but I could hear an echo of Enid.

I said once again how marvellous I thought she was being and rang off.

I was still standing beside the phone when Michael came in a few moments later. I told him briefly what had happened.

'Goodness, how gruesome, poor old Enid. Will they be buried in the same grave?'

'I don't know, I suppose so. It really is awful that both of them should have gone and both so violently.'

'Do they know what caused the fire?'

'Geraldine didn't say. Faulty wiring, I suppose, it usually is in old houses like that.'

'I'd have thought that Adrian Palgrave would have had the place gutted and thoroughly modernized. Didn't he rather fancy himself as an interior designer?'

'Well, yes,' I said, remembering the Old Schoolhouse, a nineteenth-century Gothic gem that Adrian had furnished with a veritable riot of Victoriana. 'Oh, well. No doubt we'll hear soon enough how it all happened.'

I heard the next morning. I was just boning out a smoked haddock to make some kedgeree for supper when the telephone rang and it was Roger.

'Sheila? Have you heard about Enid Palgrave?'

'Yes, isn't it dreadful! And how awful that there should have been this terrible accident so soon after Adrian's murder.'

'I'm afraid it's worse than that. The fire wasn't an accident, it was started deliberately. Enid Palgrave was murdered, too.'

For a moment I didn't really take in what Roger had said, then it suddenly hit me.

'But why? Who on earth would want to murder Enid?'

'I can only imagine that the two murders are connected. Perhaps she saw something or *knew* something that would have identified the killer.'

'But she never said anything to the police?'

'She may not have realized what she knew,' Roger said.

'No, I suppose not.'

'The reason I'm ringing,' Roger said, 'apart from putting you in the picture, is because Geraldine Marwick said that you were expecting Enid to call on you yesterday.'

I explained what had happened and why Enid wanted to see me.

'But she didn't tell you that she was going to stay overnight at the Old Schoolhouse?'

'No, I had no idea. From what Geraldine said, it sounds as if it was a sort of spur of the moment thing.'

'That's what I gathered, too. So who knew that she would be there when they started that fire?'

'Well, Geraldine . . . but that's impossible, she's devoted to Enid. But I suppose she might have told other people.'

'I did ask her and she's a bit vague. She says she mentioned it to various people she met when she went to a meeting of the Archaeological Society – apparently Enid should have gone with her – so that opens things up a bit. I must get a list of the people who were there.'

'Sally's a member,' I said, 'and Oliver goes when he's down here.' I hesitated. 'So does Will. Oh, and Eleanor, of course, and Father Freddy, everyone, really.'

'You didn't go yourself?'

'No, I felt a bit headachey and it wasn't anything I was particularly interested in.'

'Pity, I'll ring Jack and Rosemary, perhaps they went and can remember who was there.'

'Roger, how do you know that the fire was deliberate?'

'It was started by some rags soaked in petrol pushed through the letter-box. If you remember it's a large opening, some sort of Victorian ironwork thing. It's quite easy to get your whole hand through it, so whoever it was could reach through and set the rags alight.'

'Do you know when all this happened?'

'Well, the farmer down the road saw the flames at about four thirty in the morning. He'd just got up for early milking. So the fire chief reckons the fire must have been set at about three to three thirty.'

'And nobody heard a car or saw anything?'

'It's a bit tucked away down that lane. Just the Old Schoolhouse, the Methodist chapel and the farm. And that lay-by just before you get to the turning is screened from the road by bushes, so you could easily park a car there without being seen.'

'But *must* it have been a murder attempt? Couldn't it just have been a particularly nasty piece of vandalism? If someone thought the house was empty . . .'

'That's obviously a possibility. But it does seem the most extraordinary coincidence, you must admit.'

'I suppose so.

'You don't sound convinced.'

'Well it does seem to be the most peculiar way to kill someone, especially if it was obvious that the fire was started deliberately.'

'The murderer might not have expected that. After all, the fire didn't spread as fiercely as it could have done. He might have thought that the rags would have been consumed in the flames. It was quite by accident that some scraps of the rag got blown to one side by the draught of the fire and preserved for us to find.'

'Yes,' I said uncertainly. 'You could be right. So I

suppose that means *another* inquest. Poor Geraldine is going to find it very difficult to get the funerals sorted out. Did you know, she's taken on all the arrangements.'

'Yes, I did gather that she'd taken charge – somewhat to the annoyance, I believe, of Enid's other friend Evelyn Page.'

I laughed. 'That's Taviscombe for you. Umbrage taken, even at a time like this!' As I went back to my haddock I tried to imagine why on earth anyone should have wanted to murder Enid. What *could* she have seen or known that made her so dangerous to someone? Perhaps, I thought suddenly, she had known about her husband's extra-marital affairs. I was sure that she would never have challenged Adrian about them because she would have been afraid of losing him. But now she might have realized that they could somehow have been a motive for his murder. If she *knew* that Adrian had been the man Lucy Maxwell had been so tragically in love with, then she might have thought that Will . . . I resolutely made my mind a blank and went on chopping up hard-boiled eggs.

When Michael came home I told him about Roger's phone call.

'*Another* murder! A bit far-fetched, isn't it?' he said.

'That's what I thought at first, but it does make a kind of sense.'

'Oh well, it lets you off the hook about those papers she wanted you to help her with.'

'Yes,' I agreed, 'but it's hardly the way I would have wanted it to happen. I suppose they were all burned in the fire so now *nobody* will be editing them. It's a great pity, they were really very important.'

Michael leaned forward to scrape out the remains of the kedgeree from the dish.

'How come Adrian Palgrave had them in the house, anyway?' he asked. 'Surely, if they were that important, they should have been in some library or a bank vault or something?'

'There were no relatives,' I replied, 'and, as Meredith's literary executor, Adrian had the right to dispose of the papers as he thought best. I believe he was going to sell them to an American university when he'd finished all the books and articles he proposed to get out of them.'

'Were they valuable, then? In money terms, I mean?'

'Well,' I said, cutting a slice of cheesecake and pushing it towards him, 'I didn't have the chance to examine them, but there was a lot of stuff from Hemingway and Scott Fitzgerald and all those other twenties American literary expats, and American libraries still pay a lot for that sort of thing. And if there was anything *new* (and there might have been) then, yes, they would be quite valuable. I suppose they're insured, but that's not the point.'

'How did Adrian Palgrave get to be made Meredith's literary executor, anyway?'

'He'd done a book on Scott Fitzgerald and went out there to see Meredith. It seems that he made himself agreeable, very agreeable, and simply talked the old man into it. He could be a great charmer, you know, when he set his mind to it, and with someone who liked a lot of flattery he went down very well indeed.'

'Well, it didn't do him much good in the end.'

'No, poor Adrian. It really would have made his name, his big chance, you might say, to be recognized as a first-class biographer. I've never cared for his poetry, but his biographies were excellent. He would have done a good job on Meredith. Which is more than poor Enid would have done. From a purely literary point of view it's just as well she never got her hands on that material. She'd have made a dreadful dog's breakfast of it!'

'Perhaps some public-minded literary critic did away with her to preserve Meredith's reputation,' Michael said.

'There could be worse motives for murder,' I agreed. 'Can you finish this up? I hate having bits left over.'

Chapter Ten

Rosemary is a member of the Garden Club and I had promised to go as her guest on an outing to the Margery Fish garden at East Lambourne. To be honest, I really didn't feel like going anywhere, but I knew she'd be disappointed if I dropped out. Anyway, I thought that a little communing with Nature might stop me squirrelling about in my mind about the two deaths. In a way, Enid's death had made me quite sure that Will was not the murderer. I could just about see him striking Adrian down in a blind rage, as some sort of revenge for Lucy, but there was no way that he could ever have tried to burn poor Enid alive. Indeed, of all the people who might be considered suspects, there was no one, I felt, capable of such vicious brutality.

In the coach, trundling along the narrow lanes, Rosemary was inclined to the same view.

'Well, I don't see how it *can* have been murder, not this time. I think Roger's got a bit carried away, don't you? I mean, can you see anyone *we* know doing a thing like that!'

'No, I can't,' I replied. 'I still think it was vandals. After all, there was that business last year when those young boys tried to burn down the sports pavilion at the school.'

'Exactly!' Rosemary shook her head vehemently. 'I blame the teachers really, and the parents – no sort of discipline. Children nowadays seem to think they can get away with anything. Well, they can, if you think of it. All those boys got was a warning and a few hours' community service, whatever *that* might mean.'

'I think they do things in hospitals and for the old people,' I said.

'Well, I wouldn't like to think of any old people of mine having anything to do with young tearaways like that!'

'Arson,' I said reflectively, 'always seems to be a particularly *rural* crime – rick-burning and all that sort of thing.'

We considered this thought for a moment and then Rosemary said, 'Well, anyway, they won't be able to say this is Robin's fault.'

'I suppose not,' I said slowly, 'though, of course, we don't know where he actually *is*. He may have gone to ground somewhere locally.'

'You know Taviscombe,' Rosemary said. 'You can't imagine that *somebody* wouldn't have seen him by now if he was anywhere in the neighbourhood.'

I agreed that it was virtually impossible to disappear in the countryside where every unusual occurrence is carefully monitored.

'Though even if he had gone quite a long way away,' I said, 'he could still have come back.' I mean, he had his car. I don't suppose the police have found that?'

'No, he seems to have vanished off the face of the earth. Poor Robin.' Rosemary looked anxious. 'I do wish I knew what had happened to him. He must be in a dreadful state to have gone off like that. I'm so afraid he may have done something silly.'

'You mean . . .'

'Well, he did try to commit suicide when he was, you know, having that breakdown. I don't think it was a really serious attempt, just a cry for help, as they say. He took an overdose of aspirin and they got him to hospital in time and pumped him out. But now . . .'

'The police are looking for him. I'm sure they'll find him soon,' I said reassuringly.

'But what use will that be,' Rosemary asked in exasperation, 'if they charge him with murder!'

Mrs Browning, the President of the club, came down the aisle towards us, swaying slightly with the movement of the coach.

'Hello, Sheila,' she said, 'so glad that you could come. We do need to fill up the coach every time to make it a practical proposition and today several people simply haven't turned up! It's really too bad!'

'Oh, goodness,' Rosemary said, 'I meant to tell you but I forgot. Eleanor sends her apologies but she's really seedy and couldn't make it. I think she's got this wretched summer flu, there's a lot of it about.'

Mrs Browning didn't appear to be mollified by this explanation.

'Well, I do think she might have let me know in good time. If only I'd known there was a seat to spare, old Mrs Burns very much wanted to come. Her husband was a great gardener, you know . . .' She moved back up the aisle still complaining.

'*Oh* dear,' Rosemary said. 'Now she'll be offended all afternoon. It completely went out of my mind. I saw Jessie in the library yesterday and she told me then and I said I'd tell Mrs Browning.'

'Poor Eleanor,' I said, 'is she in bed?'

'Yes, Jessie said she was really poorly. Mind you, I thought Jessie looked a bit off-colour herself. I hope she doesn't get it too. I know Mrs Carter comes in every day, but with a house that size *and* two invalids . . . I'll ring up when we get back and see if there's anything I can do.'

The old Manor House and its beautiful gardens exercised a tranquillizing effect upon us both. The sun had come out and it was a really perfect English summer's day. The glorious profusion of plants, arranged apparently haphazardly, but actually with so much care and imagination, rested the mind and lifted the spirits.

'Just look at those gorgeous spurges!' Rosemary said. 'We've got a couple in the garden but they look positively *mingy* compared with those. I wonder what variety they are?'

She moved away to examine them more closely and I drifted on to look at a particularly fine tree peony. As I stood beside it, admiring the great yellow stamens and the velvety crimson petals, like some Oriental painting, I was aware of a conversation just on the other side of the shrubbery. Dorothy Browning's voice had that loudness and clarity that makes it impossible *not* to listen to what she is saying, whether you want to or not.

'Yes, it *was* a dreadful thing! Young hooligans! I don't know what the police are thinking of to let such things happen. Poor Enid! She *was* a difficult woman, I know – well, you remember that time when the Club was on *Gardener's Question Time* and she tried to hog all the limelight, just because her husband was something at the BBC. I don't for a moment believe he had anything to do with our being chosen!'

There was an inaudible murmur from her companion and she went on, '*He* was a nasty piece of work! Yes, I know some people said he had a certain kind of charm, but I never thought he was – how shall I put it? – *trustworthy*. I believe *she* had a great deal to put up with. What? Oh, *women*, dear, other women! As a matter of fact . . .' Here she lowered her voice and I was forced to crane forward, hoping that the bulk of a large syringa would hide me, to catch what she was saying. 'I know something of the matter myself. I was going out to see Madge Frisby – she's got a most unusual escallonia, a white one, and she promised me some cuttings – so I was driving through that wooded road to Upper Combe when I saw a car parked just off the road. I recognized it at once as Adrian Palgrave's because he gave Doris and me a lift back when we all went to that open day at Bridgecroft Manor. I had to slow down, because there's that very sharp bend just there, so I could see quite clearly who was in the car.'

She paused for dramatic effect and to my dismay I saw Rosemary coming towards me, about to say something. I put my finger to my lips (feeling idiotically histrionic as I did so) and flapped my hand up and down to implore silence. She made a face at me and stood stock still, while Dorothy Browning's voice rang out clearly.

'Adrian Palgrave was in that car with a woman! I don't know who she was – dark, a high complexion, rather gypsyish – but they were talking very earnestly, very earnestly indeed! They were so absorbed with each other that I don't believe they even *heard* my car until I'd gone by!'

Rosemary raised her eyebrows and made another face and I waited hopefully for more revelations but, alas, a group of gardening enthusiasts came up and began talking about a special sort of *Eucryphia* on the other side of the garden and they all drifted away.

'Well!' Rosemary said, her eyes sparkling. 'What was all that about?'

'Adrian's "goings on",' I said. 'Seen in a car with a woman!'

'Trust Dorothy Browning to think the worst,' Rosemary snorted. 'Mind you, there probably *was* something in it, knowing Adrian. I wonder who it was?'

'Dark, high complexion, rather gypsyish,' I repeated. 'No one comes to mind.'

Rosemary thought for a minute and said regretfully, 'No, I can't think of anyone. Besides, I'd have thought he'd keep all that sort of thing for London. You know what people are like down here, Enid would have heard about it in no time.'

'Perhaps she did,' I said. 'I don't suppose she'd have done anything about it. She'd never have divorced him.'

'Poor Enid,' Rosemary said thoughtfully, 'it must have been pretty awful for her, if you come to think of it, everyone knowing that Adrian only married her for her money.'

'I suppose she was lucky to have money to be married *for*,' I said sardonically. A sudden thought struck me.

'I wonder who'll get it all?' I asked. 'The money, I mean. They neither of them had any close relations. Geraldine said that there's a cousin of Adrian's in New Zealand, or something. I suppose he'll get the lot.'

'Perhaps he came over here in disguise and bumped them both off,' Rosemary suggested frivolously.

I laughed, but in the coach going home I took with me not only a pot of species geranium (*G. pratense* 'album') but also several new thoughts about Adrian's murder.

It was quite late when we got back and I found that Michael had got his own supper.

'I thought it would save you the bother,' he said virtuously.

I looked round the kitchen, noting with resignation what appeared to be the entire contents of the fridge scattered over the work-top, the eggshells in the sink, the crumbs spilling off the bread board on to the floor, and the unbelievable number of dirty bowls and pans Michael seemed to require for the construction of a simple dish of bacon and eggs.

'That was very thoughtful of you,' I said as I filled the kettle. 'Do you want a cup of coffee?'

'Please. I say, Ma, Edward asked me to ask you if you could do us a favour?'

I reflected that Michael now seemed to think of himself as very much a part of the firm and I thought how pleased Peter would have been.

'Yes, of course, darling. What is it?'

'Well, you know old Thompson – Forsyth and Merrick – he's the Palgraves' solicitor, and he's a bit worried about those Meredith papers. Like you said, they're pretty valuable and quite a lot of them were burned in the fire, but some survived. Thompson wondered if you'd have a look at them – you being Literary and all that – and see if you could let him know what's left, if you see what I mean.'

I screwed the top back on to a bottle of cooking oil and replaced it on the shelf.

104

'Well, I suppose I could have a look. But of course I don't know what was there originally, so it'll be a bit difficult to know what's gone. How much stuff is there, do you know?'

'Haven't a clue, Thompson didn't give us any details. He just wanted to know if you'd look through them.'

'OK. Tell him I will. Here's your coffee. There's a banana cake if you want some.'

'No thanks, I must dash. I'm supposed to be playing badminton with Gerry in half an hour.'

I sat down at the kitchen table and drank my cup of coffee slowly, thinking about Adrian's work on the Meredith papers and wondering just how much he had done. My meditations were interrupted by Michael appearing dramatically in the doorway with a garment in his hand. 'Ma, there's no buttons on this shirt and I need it this evening!'

'If only you'd *keep* the buttons when they come off, I could sew them on for you,' I said, with what I felt was admirable restraint.

'Oh, you know how they always pop off when you're not looking,' Michael said airily, handing over the offending shirt.

I went upstairs, rummaged in my sewing box to find three buttons of approximately the right size and colour, and began to sew them on.

When Michael had gone and all was peaceful again I had my own supper and reduced the kitchen to order again. The pot with the species geranium caught my eye and I thought I would go into the garden to see where I would like to plant it.

It was a quiet evening with no wind and the beginnings of a brilliant sunset. I wandered around the garden with the pot in one hand and a trowel in the other, the dogs trotting hopefully beside me in case I was thinking of taking a walk. I bent down to dig a hole at the end of one of the raised beds and Foss strolled across the garden to watch my efforts critically. I had just smoothed the earth round the new plant when I heard the telephone ringing. I dropped the trowel and made a dash for the house. It was Roger.

'Sheila, I thought you ought to know, Robin Turner's dead.'

'Oh no!'

'Rosemary's pretty upset, as you can imagine, and Jack's away on business so I thought you might have a word with her.'

'But what happened? How did he die? Where has he been?'

'They fished his body out of the water at Bristol Dock.'

'Bristol! What on earth was he doing there!'

'I can't say. I haven't had the details yet, just the bare fact. I'm going down almost immediately. I had to tell Rosemary straight away; she and Jack were the closest to him. He didn't have any family.'

'Oh, poor Robin.' I still hadn't really taken it in. A thought struck me. 'Is this another murder, Roger?'

'I honestly don't know. It could be, I suppose, or perhaps suicide.'

'You mean . . .'

'If he was responsible for the other murders. Yes, well, it's possible. But we won't know anything for sure until they've done the autopsy.'

'Yes, of course.'

'I must go now. If you *could* ring Rosemary, she's in a bit of a state.'

I sat for a few moments collecting my thoughts before I picked up the phone and spoke to Rosemary.

We talked round and round, coming to no conclusion. Indeed, how could we? But I felt it was a good thing to let her talk it out.

'I can't understand why *Bristol*,' she kept saying. 'He didn't know anyone there.'

'Perhaps that's why,' I said. 'If he wanted to get away.'

'But *why* should he want to get away?'

'Well, I suppose . . .'

'No, I *can't* believe he killed Adrian and Enid, especially not in that awful way. You know what a gentle person he is . . . he was.'

She was near to tears and there seemed nothing that I could say that would be of any comfort.

'Shall I come round?' I asked.

'No, bless you, I'm all right. Jilly phoned and Jack will be back tomorrow. I had a word with him on the phone. He couldn't believe it, either. It's just that it keeps going round and round in my head. I can't think of anything else.'

I found that I couldn't concentrate on anything, either. Theories, speculations, conjectures, they were all of them useless until we had more information. But that didn't stop my mind formulating and rejecting them. *If* Robin had killed Adrian and *if* Enid had somehow found out then he would have had to kill her – but in such a way? He may have had the wild idea of making it look like an accident and then, realizing just what he had done, felt he couldn't live with himself. Poor Robin.

I suddenly thought of Eleanor. I must let her know. She would be devastated, since she and Robin had become so close. Reluctantly I picked up the phone. It rang for quite some time and then I heard Jessie's voice, hesitant and cautious.

'Yes? Who is it?'

'Jessie, it's Sheila Malory. Is Miss Eleanor there?'

'She's not well, Mrs Malory, she's in bed.'

'Oh, I am sorry. I had hoped she would be feeling better by now. The thing is, I've got some bad news for her.'

'Bad news?' Jessie's soft voice was sharpened by alarm. 'What bad news?'

'It's Mr Turner, I'm afraid he's dead.'

There was a long silence, then she said, 'This will be terrible news for Miss Eleanor. Poor soul, she's been so upset, like, over Mrs Palgrave, and now this!'

'Yes, I know, it's really awful.'

107

'Was it a car accident?' Jessie asked.

'No. No, he was drowned. They found him in Bristol Dock.'

'Deu! What was he doing in Bristol, the poor young man?'

'We don't know, Jessie.'

'Mr Robin hadn't any call to go to *Bristol*.' Jessie made it sound like Siberia. 'He knows he has friends here.'

'Yes, he had a lot of friends in Taviscombe.'

'I can't tell Miss Eleanor tonight, she's been really poorly all day. She needs to get a good night's rest. I'll see she takes some of those pills to make her sleep.'

'Yes, you will know what is best.' I felt relieved in a cowardly way that I didn't have to break the news to Eleanor myself. 'She's very lucky to have you to take such good care of her, Jessie.'

'Well, we take care of each other,' Jessie replied. 'She's very good to me, Mrs Malory. I owe her a lot, more than I can ever repay.'

'Well, I'm sure she appreciates all you do,' I said. 'I hope,' I added, 'that *you* haven't caught this flu thing too. You didn't look too well when I saw you at Dr Macdonald's.'

'There's nothing wrong with me!' Jessie spoke vehemently.

'Well, if you do feel a bit seedy, do take care of yourself. And do let me know if there is anything I can do, won't you? Shopping or anything like that, if you can't get out.'

'That's very kind of you, Mrs Malory, but we can manage very well.'

Poor Eleanor, I thought as I put the phone down, just when she had something to brighten her life it's snatched away from her. Jessie had sounded rather strange, though after all that had happened at Kinsford and then Enid's death, I supposed it was only to be expected. And now Robin. So many awful things seemed to have been happening lately.

'One woe doth tread upon another's heels,' I said to Tris, who had followed me back into the house. He looked at me, his head on one side, puzzled by the tone of my voice. I bent down and patted him.

'No, it's all right,' I said. 'I'm only talking to myself.'

It was getting dark and I went to draw the curtains in the sitting room. In the twilight I could just make out the small figure of Foss, busily digging his own hole in the newly turned earth around my geranium.

Chapter Eleven

There was no word from Roger the next day, or the day after. I rang Rosemary who said that Jilly had told her that Roger was still in Bristol.

'Apparently there are several things besides . . . besides Robin, that he has to see to there. So we don't know anything more. Sheila, do you think that Robin might have *known* something and was frightened that the murderer would find out? And *that's* why he ran away like that to hide, somewhere he couldn't be found.'

'And the murderer *did* find him,' I said slowly, 'and killed him to stop him telling the police what he knew. Well, it certainly makes more sense than thinking of Robin as the murderer.'

'That's what Jack says,' Rosemary replied. 'And it does fit in.'

'But why,' I asked, 'didn't Robin just go to the police and *tell* them?'

'Well, you know what Robin was like, such a nervy sort of person. I'm sure he thought the police suspected *him* and he might have felt they wouldn't believe him if he told them that someone else killed Adrian and Enid.'

We worried away at the subject for a little while and then I said, 'I rang Eleanor, but she was ill in bed so Jessie said she'd tell her.'

'Oh, Eleanor!' Rosemary exclaimed. 'How awful of me! I was so taken up with how badly *we* felt that I totally forgot about her! She'll miss him dreadfully, they'd become very close. Jack used to tease me, he said that

110

she was his mother-figure now! But honestly, I was so glad for both of them. Poor Eleanor, she doesn't have much luck with the people she loves. First she lost Phyllis – that was tragic, too – and then Sir Ernest died, and she was so devoted to him, and now, just when she seemed to have taken on a new lease of life, poor Robin goes too.'

'I know,' I replied. 'She seems to have everything anyone could want, that marvellous house and plenty of money to keep it up, but she's been pretty lonely these last few years, even though she joins in with all sorts of things. She's got no one special, no family, no particular friend. Anyway,' I continued, 'I thought I'd just pop over there today and see how she is.'

'Oh dear, I'd meant to go a couple of days ago, but somehow I haven't got round to it. Mother's just decided that she wants a new television set and we've had the man from Taviscombe Electrics back and forth half a dozen times because she isn't satisfied about the picture. And *I've* got to be there every time so that she can communicate with the poor man through me: "Tell him that it's too bright now and the sound is all blurred." Honestly, Sheila, she gets worse by the day! I suppose she's bored because she doesn't feel well enough to go out. I do feel guilty about Eleanor, though.'

'For goodness' sake! You do quite enough as it is. No, I'll go along today. I don't think I'll phone first, though. I have the feeling that Jessie would try to put me off. She was being very protective the other evening when I rang.'

'She does like to *guard* Eleanor,' Rosemary said. 'She's much more like a nanny than a housekeeper, though she's much younger than Eleanor. How old would you say she is?'

'Jessie? Oh, I don't know – in her late thirties, I suppose. It's difficult to say, she always looks so *old-fashioned*, if you know what I mean.'

Jessie was looking particularly old-fashioned when she

opened the door to me the next day. She was wearing one of those full-length, rather voluminous, floral wraparound overalls that you only see nowadays in television plays about Northern Life in the thirties. I wondered where she had got it from.

'Oh, Mrs Malory. I thought you were the fish.'

She stood hesitantly in the doorway, obviously wondering whether to let me in. I felt, resentfully, that she was taking rather a lot on herself when I heard a voice behind her calling out, 'Who is it, Jessie?' and Eleanor herself appeared.

'Sheila! What a super surprise! Come in. Jessie, go and get us some coffee.'

She led me into the morning room where there was a fire burning, although it was quite a warm day and the room was flooded with sunlight. As we sat down and the light fell on Eleanor's face, I was shocked to see how ill she looked.

'Eleanor, my dear,' I said impulsively, 'you look dreadful! Have you seen Dr Macdonald?'

She gave a little laugh.

'Oh, you know me! Tough as old boots! Just a touch of flu. I'll be right as rain tomorrow.'

'Still,' I said doubtfully, 'I'm sure you ought to be having antibiotics or something.'

Jessie bought in a tray of coffee and biscuits and I thought that she too looked ill; her usual rosy complexion had faded to a sort of putty colour. When she had gone, I said, 'Jessie looks very poorly, too. How is she? I saw her in Dr Macdonald's waiting-room the other day.'

'Poor Jessie, she's had one of those beastly gastric things and they do pull you down.'

'That's one of the reasons I called, really,' I said. 'With you both being ill, I wondered if there was anything I could do – shopping or something.'

'Bless you, that is kind! But no, we're OK. Mrs Carter from the village comes in every day and we're managing quite nicely.'

'The other reason I came,' I said tentatively, 'is to say how very sorry I was to hear about Robin.'

Eleanor's hand trembled and the cup she was holding rattled in its saucer.

'I just don't *understand*. Why did he go away like that? I thought he knew that we were his friends, that we *cared* about him. And he just went without a word . . . And then, to die like that . . .' Her voice broke. 'Sorry,' she said, dabbing at her eyes with a handkerchief, 'I'm making an awful fool of myself.'

'No, no,' I said soothingly, 'you're still in a state of shock, and you must still feel rotten from the flu. Anyway,' I went on, 'everything's been so awful lately. First Adrian, then Enid, and now Robin.'

'Enid!' Eleanor's face crumpled grotesquely. 'That was dreadful, dreadful! If only she'd never gone home like that, if only she'd stayed with Geraldine, it would never have happened. And now Robin's gone. I've lost him forever . . .'

She was crying now, tears pouring down her face unchecked, the handkerchief twisting between her fingers.

I got up and knelt down beside her and put my arm round her should. '*Please* don't distress yourself like this, it's not good for you.'

Jessie, coming back into the room to collect the tray, looked at me accusingly.

'She shouldn't be upset like this, not when's she's not herself.'

I stood up guiltily.

'I'm sorry,' I said inadequately, 'I shouldn't have spoken about Enid and Robin.'

Jessie crossed over and gently helped Eleanor from her chair.

'Come along, cariad,' she said gently, 'what you need is a nice lie-down.' She led her from the room and I was alone.

I felt dreadful that my tactlessness had distressed

Eleanor so much. I also felt embarrassed, as we do when someone we've always thought of as jolly and extrovert – almost a comic figure – suddenly reveals deep and real emotions. I'd never known Eleanor cry before, in all the years I'd known her. Not even when Phyllis died so tragically. Of course I'd been away when Sir Ernest died and I remembered now that my mother had been very worried about her then, because she had taken his death so hard. She had, indeed, been ill for several weeks.

I left, closing the heavy door behind me, and drove away without looking back at the house. I was shaken by the intensity of the emotion I'd just witnessed. Poor Eleanor – her last chance of happiness gone. When we're young we feel that nothing will ever hurt as much as the griefs we feel then, but the pain of middle-age is sharper and cuts deeper, accentuated by our knowledge that there is now so little time left.

I drove down the road into the village and pulled into the lay-by beside the church to recover myself a little before driving on.

After a few moments I became aware that there was a certain amount of activity going on in the church, people coming and going. I wondered vaguely if it was a special service – Father Freddy is a great one for Days of Obligation and so forth. Looking up I saw a handwritten poster pinned to the church notice board announcing a Flower Festival in aid of the Organ Refurbishment Fund. Looking at flowers seemed a reasonable way to restore my spirits, so I got out of the car and made my way up the steep path to the church.

St Decumen's is a splendid building, disproportionately large, as many Somerset churches are, for the area it serves. It is set in a well-kept churchyard with many fine tombs and monuments. Just by the church door, next to an old eighteenth-century monument embellished with urns and carved swags, stood a large granite cross to the memory of Sir Ernest, with a mass of fresh flowers at its base. I paused to look at it, thinking that Jessie must have brought the flowers since Eleanor was ill. As I stood there, a door at the side of the church was opened revealing a dank, cavernous space where mowers and watering-cans and such-like things were kept, and the tall figure of Father Freddy emerged. When he saw me he came down the path, talking rapidly in his loud, booming voice.

'Sheila, dear child, what a pleasure to see you! I have just been inspecting the *tap*. Apparently it won't turn off properly, so our worthy Greene has been telling me, and it is *dripping* all over the floor. Most distressing. He says it needs a new *washer* or some such device, but I am, alas, ignorant of all things mechanical and was quite unable to be of any *assistance*.'

'Oh dear,' I said, rather put out at this form of greeting. 'What will you do?'

'I, dear child? *I* will do nothing. Greene, however, seems to have the matter well in hand and proposes to *replace* the washer with a new one. So our problem will be solved. I believe,' he continued with a smile, 'he only wished to inform me of the disaster so that I might admire the excellent way he was coping with the situation. Well now, how are you? Have you come to visit our Flower Festival?'

I explained that I'd just come from seeing Eleanor and had come upon the Festival quite by chance.

He looked grave.

'Ah yes, Eleanor. I fear she is not at all well, very much *not* her usual ebullient self. I was there yesterday and heard the sad news from her about young Robin, poor boy!'

'She's very upset – Robin and Enid – and Adrian, of course. It must have been a dreadful strain on her.'

'Indeed, Taviscombe and its environs has been a positive *charnel*-house, quite like the *worst* excesses of Jacobean tragedy.'

In anyone else this flippancy would have been distasteful, but it was so typical of Father Freddy's manner of speech that one accepted it.

'I wish she'd see a doctor,' I said. 'She looks awful. And Jessie's not much better. They are both of them quite ill.'

'Indeed? I hadn't realized that Jessie was also unwell. She had created a truly memorable orange cake yesterday – I must say I did make something of a *pig* of myself, I am ashamed to say. It was imperceptive of me not to have noticed that she, too, was not herself.'

'Jessie seems to be well enough to look after Eleanor, thank goodness. She really is a treasure.'

'Indeed. I have often *envied* Eleanor, sinful though that undoubtedly is. My own Mrs Darby is, as you know, a very worthy soul, but her idea of *haute cuisine* is shepherd's pie followed by jam roll and *custard!*'

'You would prefer moussaka followed by apricot roulade!' I laughed.

'*Touché!* There is, of course, a great deal to be said for classic English cooking. Not *quite* as classic as some of those unappetizing Elizabethan recipes that poor Enid was wont to make so much of in her little books, but a jugged hare, for example – properly done in a really good port wine – or a decently hung rib of beef. And,' – he leaned towards me confidentially as if imparting some very important secret – 'I really do believe that I actually *prefer* a properly made English apple pie (with clotted cream, of course) to our French cousins' *tarte aux pommes.*' He stood back and looked at me hard, to see how I had taken this daring statement.

'I quite agree,' I said as solemnly as I could.

I began to move towards the main door of the church and he walked beside me, his long cassock flapping slightly in a breeze that had sprung up. 'A Flower Festival,' he mused, 'a festival of flowers. In some ways that sounds almost *pagan*, does it not? And yet, we are told to consider the lilies of the field.' He gestured towards a great vase of regale lilies that were sending out waves of rich perfume, even in the cool of the church. 'Though I believe that those mentioned in the Scriptures were a kind of anemone, is that not so?'

'How beautiful it all is!' I exclaimed. And indeed the church was magnificently decorated with a multitude of flowers, from the great formal arrangements of lilies, delphiniums, and paeonies to tiny bunches of wild flowers packed along the ledges of the great windows. We walked slowly down the nave admiring the various decorations.

'So much work!' I said, 'and all so beautifully done. You're very lucky to have such talent in the parish.'

'Indeed, the village is immensely fortunate to have such a high proportion of excellent women, all of whom, I am glad to say, are most enthusiastic about such things. My own Mrs Darby is particularly assiduous. Although her *cooking* may leave much to be desired, I am most fortunate in that particular respect, her appetite for parish work appears to be unlimited. A celibate priest, my dear Sheila, as you may imagine, can sometimes be at a disadvantage, lacking as he does a wife, or *helpmeet* to share some of the more mundane duties of his office.'

'Good gracious!' I interrupted him. 'Can that possibly be bougainvillaea and plumbago round the pulpit!'

'Ah yes.' Father Freddy smiled with simple pleasure. 'To be sure. Our exotica, delightful, are they not? Kind Eleanor had them sent over. They are in their pots, of course, and we have tried to put them as near as possible to some source of *heat* since they are very delicate.'

He bent down and moved the large pot a little nearer to one of the radiators.

'Can you manage?' I asked anxiously, 'That pot looks very heavy.'

'Not at all, dear child.' He brushed the dirt off his hands and stood up.

'I don't think I've ever seen them at Kinsford,' I said.

'They remain in the largest of the greenhouses,' Father Freddy said, 'and I believe that they have done very well and multiplied. Sir Ernest, of course, planted the originals, I imagine as a reminder of his early years in the consular service in the South of France. Cannes, was it, or Nice? Somewhere agreeable, I know.'

'How gorgeous. They are the most immensely evocative plants, aren't they?' I touched a purple bract with the tip of my finger. 'It does make one nostalgic for the sun and the sea and masses of these marvellous things tumbling down from balconies.'

'And the smell of the lavender fields at Grasse!' Father Freddy agreed. 'And,' he continued with even more enthusiasm, 'the smell of newly baked brioches and that wonderful *soupe aux poissons* with aïoli! Ah, the days of our youth!'

We both stood for a moment in a pleasant glow of nostalgia, which was broken by the approach of a small, grey-haired woman in a tweed suit and squashed felt hat, whom I recognised as his house-keeper Mrs Darby.

'Sorry to disturb you, Father,' she said, and then broke off to greet me. 'Why, if it isn't Mrs Malory? How nice to see you here. Are you enjoying the flowers?' She recollected herself and turned back. 'There's a message for you, Father, from the Bishop. So I thought I'd better come down to the church and find you in case it's important. Well, *anything* from the Bishop's important really, if you see what I mean. He wants you to ring him as soon as possible. I thought it might be some sort of *emergency*, "as soon as possible". So I thought you ought to know right away.'

Father Freddy smiled vaguely at her and said, 'Yes, indeed, you did quite right, Mrs Darby, I will attend to it immediately. The Bishop! It could be *anything*, anything at all; you might let your imagination roam, Sheila.' He turned to me. 'The field is wide indeed.' He gave a little laugh, inviting me to share some esoteric clerical joke. 'I must away! Enjoy the bougainvillaea!'

He raised his arm in a gesture that combined a farewell wave and a sort of ecclesiastical blessing and moved swiftly away.

I turned to Mrs Darby. 'It's nice to see him in such good form!' I said, smiling affectionately at the tall figure making its way up the side aisle.

'He's a lovely man,' Mrs Darby said. 'I couldn't imagine St Decumen's without him!'

'No indeed, though of course he's getting on. He must be nearly eighty.'

'But very *fit*, Mrs Malory. Up every morning at seven, regular as clockwork, and often he doesn't go to bed till well after midnight. Writing that book of his.'

Father Freddy was engaged on a study of the life and times of Bishop Odon, a work of great scholarship that he had been tinkering with for the last twenty years.

'How beautiful the church looks,' I said. 'Not just the flowers, but everything is so splendidly kept. The brass! You have so much of it still.'

Indeed Father Freddy had refused to put away any of the magnificent brasses that decorated the church – the finely wrought candlesticks on the altar, the heavy, intricately engraved cross, the great eagle surmounting the lectern – saying grandly that God had His own ways of protecting His property against thieves and vandals. So far, certainly, his faith had been justified.

Mrs Darby looked gratified.

'It's beautiful brass,' she said, 'and I like to keep it nice. I do all the brasses myself, it's my special responsibility. We have rotas, of course, for the cleaning and the flowers. But the brasses are mine.'

She gave a little nod of satisfaction and pride.

'Well, they certainly do you credit, Mrs Darby,' I said. 'They really *gleam*! Look at the way those candlesticks catch the light!'

An expression of aggravation crossed her face and she leaned towards me confidentially.

'That's always been my job, Mrs Malory. It's quite understood, everyone in the parish knows that. Everyone, it seems, except a certain off-comer!'

'Oh?' I said, bracing myself to hear the usual complaints current in church-cleaning circles, where the rigidity of demarcation lines could teach the unions a thing or two.

'Mrs Forester,' she hissed, looking over her shoulder to make sure that she wasn't being overheard. 'I know that's who it was. The other week. They were just due for a clean. I rub them up every week, but they get a proper going-over, if you know what I mean, every three weeks. And she did it! I came into the church all ready to give them a really good clean, and she'd been there before me!'

'Goodness! Are you sure?'

'Oh yes, there were smears of the brass polish, not properly rubbed off. Well, I'd never leave them like that! She denied it, of course, but there's no doubt in my mind! Just because she did the brasses when she was in *Kidderminster*' – the amount of scorn and loathing that Mrs Darby put into the name was formidable – 'doesn't give her the right to do the same here!'

'No, indeed!'

Mrs Darby seemed prepared to expatiate on her grievance, but fortunately a young couple, visitors, both wearing shorts, caught her eye.

'Look at that, Mrs Malory! In the house of the Lord! I'd better just go and keep an eye on them.'

She moved away and I made my escape.

As I came out of the cool church into the warmth of the sun I felt thoroughly dazed, partly by the profusion of flowers, partly by the flow of conversation from Father Freddy and Mrs Darby. As I drove home, I slotted a tape of piano music into the cassette-player, letting the limpid notes of a Chopin Étude, each one separate and crystalline, clear my head and refresh my spirit.

Chapter Twelve

Early next morning I had a phone call from Jack.

'Look, Sheila, would you mind dropping in on Rosemary this morning? She's feeling pretty awful. We had a call from Roger last night, about Robin. It really upset her.'

'Yes, of course I will. Poor Rosemary! What about Robin?'

'It's a bit complicated; I'll leave it to Rosemary to explain. Sorry, I've got an appointment so I've got to dash. Thanks very much, Sheila.'

As soon as I decently could after breakfast I went round to Rosemary's. Her eyes were red and she looked as if she hadn't had much sleep.

'Hello, Sheila,' she said as she led me into the sitting room. 'I'm afraid everything's in a mess – I haven't even cleared away the coffee cups from last night. Hang on, let me switch the fire on; it's really chilly this morning, or is it just me?'

'No,' I said, looking out of the window at the grey, overcast sky. 'It's a miserable day and it's just started to spit with rain.'

'Did Jack ask you to come?' Rosemary demanded.

I hesitated. 'Well, yes, he did phone . . .'

'Silly old fool,' Rosemary said affectionately. 'I'm all right, really, but I'm glad you came. You'll want to know about Robin.'

'I gather you heard from Roger?'

'Yes, they've had the result of the autopsy.' Her voice

wavered slightly on the word. 'It seems that Robin had been drinking quite a lot of whisky.'

'But he hardly drinks at all!' I exclaimed.

'No, well, that's it. Roger thinks that perhaps he had too much to drink and simply fell into the water. Apparently it happened late at night, so probably no one saw him, and he just . . . drowned.'

'Oh, my dear!'

'I suppose, not being used to drink, it had an especially powerful effect.'

'Do they know why he was in Bristol?'

'Yes. They found an address in his pocket, of the small, rather grotty hotel he was staying at, down by Coronation Road. Roger went there and had a look at his things. Robin had been keeping a sort of diary, very disjointed, all about how he was sure the police were going to accuse him of Adrian's murder and how he couldn't face the thought of being locked away. There was a lot about how he felt he *had* murdered Adrian because he hated him so much – rambling stuff, Roger said. Not . . . not well balanced.'

'Roger doesn't think he *did* murder Adrian, does he?' I asked, Rosemary shook her head.

'Oh no, not if Roger's right and Enid was killed deliberately. You see, the night of the fire, Robin was in the hotel all evening. The manager saw him at about eight o'clock. He'd just come in and was, well, very drunk. He went straight up to his room. There's no way he could have driven to Taviscombe in that condition.'

'The poor boy! I suppose, if he had all these mixed-up feelings about guilt and so on, he might have . . .'

'Committed suicide, you mean?' Rosemary said. 'Yes, I suppose he might. But,' her eyes filled with tears, 'what does it *matter*? Suicide or accident, it was such an *unnecessary* death! If *only* he'd talked to me! I'm sure I could have made him see that no one who knew him would suspect *him* of such a thing!'

I thought of Eleanor and what she had said yesterday. I told Rosemary how upset she had been.

'She looked absolutely terrible,' I said, 'with that flu thing as well. Who's going to tell her about this?'

Rosemary looked stricken.

'It'll be even worse for Eleanor. Robin really meant so much to her.'

'She's been very lonely,' I replied. 'I don't think I ever realized quite *how* much until yesterday when I saw her and Jessie, rattling about in that great house! She's filled her life since Sir Ernest died, all those good works, but nobody special, no one of her own.'

'I know,' Rosemary said. 'It must be dreadful to have no family, no one really close.'

'Perhaps,' I said, 'I'll phone Father Freddy. Ask him to tell her.'

Rosemary looked doubtful.

'Do you think so? I never think of him as having any real *feelings*, if you know what I mean.'

'Yes, that rather frivolous manner can be a little off-putting and perhaps, when you get to his age, human feelings don't seem so important. But underneath I believe he's very kind. And a priest, after all, is used to doing things like that.'

A few days later, when I was on my way to tea with my friend Muriel who lives at the other end of the town, I happened to be passing the police station just as Roger was coming down the steps. I went over to greet him.

'Hello, Roger,' I said. 'How's it going?'

'Slowly, I'm afraid. Look, Sheila, I'm desperately sorry about what happened to Robin. It was the most terrible thing.'

'I know, we're all very upset.'

He hesitated for a moment, and then said, 'What is so awful is the feeling that he felt he was being persecuted. I hope I don't have to tell you that there never was any sort of harassment on our part . . .'

'No,' I said, 'we none of us felt that there was. Mind you, it's a horrid sign of the times, though, isn't it, that

123

you felt you had to say so? No,' I continued, 'I'm afraid Robin's feeling that he was being hounded was all part of his being irrational and unbalanced. I'm sure there's a clinical term for whatever was wrong with him. But as Rosemary says, it's such a *wasteful* death, so tragically unnecessary. If only he could have brought himself to *talk* to someone. Still there it is. Is there any way you can tell if it was suicide or an accident?'

'Not really,' Roger said. 'He may have been drinking to give himself courage to drown himself, or he may simply have had too much to drink and fallen in by accident. He'd been hiding away for a little while by then and was in a very confused state.'

We both stood in silence for a moment and then I said, 'Have you made any progress on the murder – or murders?'

Roger gave a little helpless shrug.

'Not really. We've all done quite a lot of leg-work, checking things out and so forth. We *did* think we'd found the murder weapon the other day. A hammer turned up in one of the litter bins on the sea-front. But it turned out to be no such thing.'

'How frustrating for you,' I said. 'So you still don't know what was used to kill poor Adrian?'

'I'm afraid not. And our chances of finding the weapon grow slimmer as time goes on. Oh yes, there is one bit of good news for you.'

'What?'

'Your friend Oliver Stevens. He does have an alibi for the time Palgrave was killed.'

'Really!' I exclaimed. 'How come?'

'Well, you know you said he came in quite a while after his wife, just before the concert started, and that he looked flustered and upset?'

'Yes?'

'I asked him about his movements and he said he'd had to send his wife on ahead because he had to wait behind for a phone call. Apparently it was from someone at the

124

BBC about a programme, so I checked with this man and it's perfectly true, he *did* phone then, so there wouldn't have been time for Stevens to go to Kinsford, murder Palgrave, and still arrive when you saw him.'

'I'm so glad,' I said, 'I really did feel like an informer when I told you about our conversation on the train. Somehow it seemed worse telling you what he'd said when he was drunk!'

Roger smiled. 'Oh, yes, and the reason Stevens was looking so upset, was that this man had told him that the project they'd discussed – spent quite a lot of time on, in fact – wasn't being taken up. So no wonder he was put out!'

'I couldn't *really* see Oliver as the murdering type,' I said. 'But then, who *is*?'

A police car drew up in the forecourt and a couple of men in uniform got out and came towards us.

'Duty calls,' Roger said. 'I must go. I'm glad I was able to set your mind at rest about Stevens.'

I turned to go and then remembered something.

'Oh, Roger, I don't know if you can tell me, but who *does* inherit all Enid's money?'

'I don't suppose it matters, my telling you. It's no one anyone here would know. The money would have gone to Palgrave, of course, but the second person named in the will was a cousin of Palgrave's in New Zealand. So no joy there. A pity – money is such a *solid* motive for murder, but this time I'm afraid it's a non-starter.'

As I went on my way, I speculated idly on the possibility of Adrian's mysterious cousin having come to England, down to Taviscombe, and to the concert, where he had somehow managed to find Adrian, strike him down, and escape by mingling with the crowd of concert-goers. I toyed with this theory for a while. It would be so much more comfortable if Adrian had been killed by someone we didn't know. But somehow the long-lost cousin idea was too far-fetched and I reluctantly abandoned it. Nevertheless, if you came to think of it, Adrian's murderer didn't *have* to be someone we all knew. He was killed in a place that was swarming with people, any one of whom might have had a reason to want him out of the way. He might have had all sorts of enemies we none of us had any idea about. I thought suddenly of the dark-haired woman that Dorothy Browning had seen him with in the car. I was quite sure that Adrian had a secret life. There may well have been other people who might want him dead.

Michael came home in the evening with a large parcel tied up with pink tape.

'Here are those Meredith papers. Edward says there's no hurry. Where do you want them?'

'Oh, put them down anywhere.'

I undid the tape and opened the parcel. There were a number of files full of papers, all giving off a slightly acrid, smoky smell. I shuddered as I looked at the scorch marks on some of them.

'I'll look at them tomorrow,' I said brusquely, bundling them back into the brown paper. 'Go and put them on my desk, will you?'

'What's the matter, Ma?' he asked as he came back into the room. 'You look a bit peculiar.'

'It was just the smell of those papers, and suddenly realizing that they'd been in the fire that killed Enid.'

'If they're going to upset you, perhaps you oughtn't to go through them. Old Thompson can find someone else to do it.'

'No,' I said, 'I was just being silly. Of course I'll look at them, I expect they'll be fascinating. Supper's nearly ready, if you want to get changed first.'

The following day I braced myself to undo the package again, wondering what I might find. Adrian had obviously done quite a lot of work on the papers. Those spread out on the desk in front of me were all letters, except for one file which contained scribbled notes for short stories. I

126

opened this one first and became so engrossed in it that I quite forgot my initial repugnance. It certainly was extraordinary to see just how selective the writer's observations had been, how he had noted down incidents and remarks which practically formed themselves into archetypal Meredith stories. Some I recognized as the originals for stories that had actually been published, some were quite unfamiliar. I thought of what Meredith scholars would make of the notes, what theories would emerge, how many theses would be written, and I felt a slight pang of disappointment that this was not my field and that I couldn't join in the fun.

As well as the noted observations there were several outlines for stories. One was about an elderly woman who had been a great beauty and how one of her former rivals took a final revenge upon her. Another was about a priest who fell hopelessly in love with a beautiful young acolyte, was disgraced, and went off to die in the mission field. Once could see, even from the sketchy notes, how Meredith would treat the themes in his own inimitable way, quite unsentimentally, the pathos subtly counterbalanced by the irony, with moments, even, of high comedy – the qualities that had made his short stories so greatly admired, finer, perhaps, than his friend and contemporary Somerset Maugham. The other files contained copies of letters that he had sent to his friends, many now famous names. Meredith had obviously conducted his correspondence with publication in mind and Adrian, as any biographer would, must have blessed the egotism of the man. The letters were all from Antibes, where Meredith spent the greater part of his life. He hardly ever came back to England after he became famous.

I read on throughout the morning, absorbed and entertained (Meredith's letters, though lacking the taut and polished style that characterized his published work, were vastly entertaining on the level of pure gossip), and only the entrance of Foss, who leapt up on to my desk with his usual demand for food, made me realize that it was lunchtime. I picked up the protesting furry body and put it down.

'No, Foss, you know you're not allowed up here! You'll just have to wait for a moment.'

As I was about to get up, my eye was caught by a letter that Foss had dislodged with his paw. Or, rather, a name, which suddenly stood out on the page. I picked up the letter and began to read.

Dearest Sybil

You, with your passion for such social minutiae (and why not, indeed), will, of course, wish to know who is gracing the Château d'Horizon at this time. Surprisingly, Maxine has a very small party and all, to my certain knowledge, tiresome bores – interior decorators, minor royalty and a strange American who drones on and on about aeroplanes.

Westminster's yacht (needless to say) is at Golfe Juan, Mrs Greville's at Cannes, both depressingly full of the usual crowd, and if one ventures into the Casino one is brought up short by the sight of Mr Selfridge scattering largesse before those two tedious girls like Jupiter and twin Danaë.

Philip and I took Beverley to the Colombe d'Or the other evening (yet *another* hideous Picasso daub on the walls) to cheer him up after Cyril had gone, and there we saw Freddy Drummond *à deux* with my gardener's son – a delightful boy, I have no doubt, and of a quite astonishing beauty, but sadly out of place in such a setting. You will be as shocked as I was, since I know you had formed a most favourable impression of Freddy's good taste. Alas, when a *grande passion* is raging, I fear the reason is often diminished. Freddy has been staying at Mougins for a couple of months and, although the villa is quite secluded, there has been a certain amount of *scandale*. My gardener's son is of an age, to be sure, but there have been others who were not and such things are not liked here. To make things worse, he is being blackmailed, most politely but quite persistently by the father of one of his inamoratos, which is really rather *sordid*, don't you agree? Freddy is a dear soul and I'm very fond of him. After all, I've known him since he first came down from Oxford – so bright and charming, the most comely theological student one could wish to meet – but he must be more discreet if we are to avoid yet another unfortunate episode. The one last year brought the English colony here under very close scrutiny which was quite *uncomfortable* for us all while it lasted.

I had a letter from H. G., to say that he is coming to Paris next month. Perhaps he will venture this far south to enliven what has been, so far, a most insipid summer.

It is always something of a shock suddenly to come upon a name one knows in unexpected circumstances and for a moment I couldn't make the connection between the Father Freddy I knew and the almost fictional figure, something out of one of Meredith's writings, of the letter. Indeed (I remembered the notes for one of the stories) he was obviously looked upon by Meredith as material for fiction.

I scrabbled among the letters looking specifically now for other references.

A thoroughly disagreeable day. We drove to Grasse – at least that was our intention – but when we had got as far as Cagnes sur Mer, a place which, as you know, I detest, the wretched motor developed some fault (do not ask me of what nature, since the internal combustion engine is as rare and strange to me as hieroglyphics in the Grand Pyramid), and so we were obliged to sit for an age in some dreary café while Chivers dealt with the problem. The situation was *not* improved by Freddy, who from ignorance, or a monumental lapse of tact, went on and on to Willie about the brilliance of Syrie's new designs. Gerald, who cannot resist making mischief, was egging him on. Willie was absolutely furious. He immediately assumed his most Chinese face and refused to speak to anyone for the rest of the afternoon. When we returned from what turned out to be a thoroughly disastrous drive, I was obliged to take a *cachet fèvre* and lie down for several hours before dinner. However, Freddy seems to have taken to heart the little lecture I gave him last week about discretion and he proposes to return to England soon, so I trust that we will be spared another scandal.

Freddy dined yesterday and we sat on the terrace looking out over the Baie des Anges at the lights of the boats on the water, perfectly idyllic. He goes back to England tomorrow and I will miss his conversation. I was somewhat disconcerted, though, when he consulted me about his religious *doubts*, a subject on which I can scarcely consider myself an expert. He appears to be considering an approach to Rome, and I was reminded of hours spent with Hugh Benson listening to many of the arguments – as tedious now as they were then. However, mellowed by an excellent dinner (did I tell you that I have a new cook? an Algerian, whose way with lamb is utter genius) I listened with exemplary patience and even gave him some excellent advice, which he will doubtless not take. I see Freddy as the chaplain of a *Cambridge* college, where his eccentricities and extravagances will be considered *refreshing* and where he will be cherished as part of an imperishable tradition. Actually, he has been offered a church just off Pont Street, which might be equally suitable and quite agreeable, if he doesn't mind drinking interminable cups of Earl Grey with doting old ladies. Indeed, it might be the very thing to provide a *cloak*, as it were, for his less conventional activities. The law is an ass, as we all know, but if one is circumspect there is no reason one should not have an enjoyable life, even in England.

That seemed to be all. I couldn't find any other references. In a kind of daze I pushed the letters back into their folders and went into the kitchen. I stood for a moment with my hands resting on the worktop, not really knowing what I was doing. I was used to the occasional mention of Father Freddy in the biographies of his contemporaries, after all he had known many famous people in his long life. But there had never been any hint of a real scandal. He was an old man now and all this had happened a long time ago. I had no way of telling how such revelations would affect him. Except – I had the knowledge of my own reaction, which was one of revulsion. The priest and the glamorous acolyte, stuff of a short story or a more sensational newspaper report, as a fiction perfectly acceptable – but in reality, somehow not. Especially with the squalid overtones of blackmail. I didn't feel that I could ever look at Freddy Drummond in quite the same light again and I had no doubt that most of his friends and parishioners would feel the same. Could he bear, could he, indeed, *afford* to let Adrian Palgrave make public events which he must have expected to be buried long since?

Foss was weaving round my ankles, butting his head against my leg.

Automatically, I reached into the fridge, got out a dish, and began to cut up some raw liver. Looking down at the red smears on my hand I suddenly smelt again Adrian's blood and remembered the red congealed to black. I dropped the scissors I was using, went over to the sink and held my hands under the tap for a long time, as if I could also wash away the memory of that horrible discovery.

Chapter Thirteen

I don't go to St James, which is the parish church of Taviscombe. The vicar is a very nice man, but his ways are not mine. Series 3 and the New English Bible were bad enough and singing familiar hymns to new, banal tunes, but what with the Kiddies' Services and guitars instead of the organ and soul music instead of the Psalms, I felt that I would be happier elsewhere. So now, like many of my generation brought up to two services every Sunday, I am no longer a regular communicant, as they say. When I do go to church I drive over to Bracken, our nearest village, where Canon Hobbes still ministers to his little flock with the help of the King James' Bible and the Book of Common Prayer. Perhaps it is wrong to want great literature as well as great spiritual teaching, but what religious faith I have is somehow inextricably bound up with the beauty of the language in which it is expressed.

St Mary's is a fine old church, built in the thirteenth century and mercifully free from Victorian restoration. As I ran my hand along the old, carved wood of the pew and looked up at the cold, pale stone I felt, as I always do, that I had somehow come home. The congregation was small and I experienced my usual pang of guilt at not coming every Sunday. On this occasion the numbers were swelled by a few holiday-makers, habitual church-goers, perhaps, or casual visitors lured in by the beauty and antiquity of the building. It was a brilliantly sunny day and light streamed in through the stained glass of the windows, making red and blue stains on the white lilies by the font. In the pew in front of me Mrs Mortimer, the churchwarden's wife, turned sharply to the east and crossed herself as she declared her affirmation of the Holy Catholick Church; one of the holiday-makers (a sandy-haired young man in jeans and a yellow short-sleeved shirt sitting across the aisle) embarked on a solitary 'for thine is the kingdom' in the second repetition of the Lord's Prayer, blushed, and fell silent; behind me, Mrs Latham in a bold contralto was declaring that 'who sweeps a room as for Thy laws makes that and th'action fine'.

I was still thinking of Herbert's splendid hymn as I sat only half listening to Canon Hobbes' sermon ('If we consider the words of the prophet Ezekiel in the context of our lives today . . .'). Certainly the ladies of St Mary's had swept and garnished their church, a very practical form of devotion, easier to give, perhaps, than a purely spiritual commitment, something I understood very well, since my sympathies will always lie with Martha rather than Mary. I looked about me. The flowers were beautifully arranged, paeans of praise to a glorious summer, and the brasses shone like gold as the sun glinted on them. The hymn was still in my head:

> 'The man that looks on glass,
> On it may stay his eye,
> Or if he pleaseth through it pass
> And then the Heavens espy.'

The gleam of the sun on the brasses. Things began to connect in my mind.

The brasses in St Decumen's, cleaned by an unknown hand, according to Mrs Darby. The candlesticks on the altar – two pairs, one large and unwieldly, but one pair smaller – one of those candlesticks might possibly have killed a man, been cleaned and put back again in a place where no one would ever think of looking for a murder weapon.

The congregation had risen and was singing again:

'Brief life is here our portion;
Brief sorrow, short-lived care.'

As I left the church I replied mechanically to Canon
Hobbes' salutation and sidestepped Mrs Mortimer, who
showed signs of wanting to engage me in conversation. I
got quickly into my car and drove home, turning over in
my mind the thought that had come to me and its possible
implications. St Decumen's was kept open during the day,
anyone could have slipped in and taken the candlestick.
If it was taken after Father Freddy had said his office for
the day and replaced before the next morning, then no
one would notice it was missing. Especially (it suddenly
occurred to me) if *both* the smaller candlesticks were
removed so that there was no obvious imbalance on the
altar to strike the casual visitor.

I was eager to put my theory to Roger, but irrationally
I felt I couldn't ring the police station on a Sunday, so I
spent a restless day unable to settle to anything. First
thing the next morning I telephoned and, to my relief, I
was connected with Roger straight away.

'Roger? It's Sheila, I've had a thought. It might be
absolutely ridiculous, but I thought I'd better tell you.'

'Sounds intriguing. What is it?'

'It's about the weapon. Do you think it might be a good
idea to test the candlesticks on the altar at St Decumen's?'

'*What*?'

I explained about Mrs Darby and the unknown cleaner.

'It *may* have been some busybody in the village,' I said,
'but somehow I can't see anyone daring to offend Mrs
Darby like that. And it would be, more or less, the one
place no one would think of looking for a murder weapon,
wouldn't it?'

'Well, yes.'

There was a pause then Roger said suddenly, 'Why
not! We've nothing to lose and we've drawn a blank
everywhere else.'

There was another silence, then he continued, 'Sheila, is there any other reason why you thought of this?'

I was silent in my turn and Roger said urgently, 'Sheila, I know you hate to feel that you're informing on people you know, but this is a very serious matter.'

'Yes,' I said, 'I know.'

'So if you've any idea, any idea at all, you really must tell me. I hope you know me well enough by now to be sure that I'll be discreet about the source of my information.'

'Yes,' I said, 'it's not that, really. It's just that what I've been thinking is so – oh, I don't know – so *unbelievable*!'

'So there *is* something else?'

'Sort of.'

And I told him what I had discovered in the Meredith papers.

'Freddy *Drummond*!' he exclaimed.

'I know,' I said. 'You see what I mean about unbelievable.'

'But he's an old man!'

'But tall, and heavily built. And strong,' I added, remembering how easily he had moved the heavy pot in the church.

'Ye-es.' Roger was obviously having the same difficulty as I had in coming to terms with my theory.

'I think he could have done it,' I said. 'If you think about it, Adrian would be totally relaxed in his company, no problem there about sitting down with his back to his assailant! If you can't trust a clergyman!'

'True,' Roger agreed. 'Drummond could have asked Palgrave to meet him before the concert to talk about the papers. They both knew Kinsford well, so that they'd have known that they could talk privately in the old dairy – though why they couldn't have discussed it at the rectory or at Palgrave's . . .'

'They probably had,' I broke in. 'I imagine that Adrian had told Father Freddy about the letters (there may have been others among those that were burnt) and said that he was going to use them in the biography. I bet he was

135

quite firm about that. No amount of pleading would have made Adrian change his mind if he thought it would spice up the biography and increase sales. Can't you just see all those juicy extracts, pre-publication, in the *Sunday Times*!'

'So this would have been a final attempt to make Palgrave change his mind?' Roger said.

'Yes.'

'And Drummond took along a heavy candlestick as a weapon, just in case he couldn't reason with him?'

'Oh dear, when you put it like that it does sound unlikely.'

'I'm not so sure. It all depends on how strongly Drummond felt about being exposed like that.'

'It was a pretty nasty episode,' I said slowly, 'and if it was going to be sensationalized . . .'

'Well, leave that to one side,' Roger said. 'What about Enid? Surely you can't think Drummond would deliberately try to burn her to death?'

'No, I'm sure he wouldn't,' I said quickly. 'But, you see, I don't expect he knew she was there. I'm sure he thought she was still staying with Geraldine. He just wanted to destroy the papers.'

'Possibly. Did you see him coming in to the concert?'

'Yes. *Yes*,' I said. 'He came in quite late, almost as it was about to start.'

I remembered the tall figure flinging off his cloak with a grand gesture.

'Goodness, yes,' I cried. 'He was wearing a cloak over his cassock – you know, the one with the lion's head clasp. He could easily have concealed one of the candlesticks under that when he met Adrian!'

There was another pause and then Roger said, 'Have you seen him since the murder?'

'Yes, that day in the church, when Mrs Darby told me about the brasses.'

'Was he there when she told you?'

'No, he'd left by then, to talk to the Bishop.'

'Good. How did he seem?'

'Just as usual, really. But, you know, I do feel sometimes that he doesn't really inhabit our world.'

'What do you mean?'

'Hard to explain. I suppose it's just that he's so very much *not* of this day and age. Well, you've met him, you must know what I mean. I think he doesn't really relate to everyday life. And he seems curiously devoid of any real feeling. He's kind and sympathetic, of course, if people come to him with their troubles, I'm sure, but I always get the impression that he's never been actually touched by any emotion himself.'

'If that's the case, why would he bother to kill Palgrave for threatening to reveal a scandal of so long ago?'

'Vanity, perhaps? An old man's final sin. He's very proud of being a local character and a famous figure. I think if everyone down here shunned him – and they probably would – he'd be quite lost. It sounds a bit odd, I know, but I think he's finally found a place for himself down here and I honestly think it would kill him to lose it.'

'You may be right,' Roger said. 'Okay, then, I'll get those candlesticks checked. Obviously, don't tell anyone what you've just told me. Oh, and hang on to those Meredith papers. I'd like to have a look at the relevant passages.'

When I had put the phone down I went into my study, put the package tied up with pink tape into the top drawer of my desk, locked it, and (feeling rather melodramatic) hid the key in a vase on the mantelpiece. Then I tried to put the whole thing out of my mind. There was nothing anyone could do now until Roger had the results of the tests on the candlesticks.

'Edward's given me the day off on Friday,' Michael said that evening as he crawled over the floor of the sitting room in search of an errant piece of feather that he was using to tie a fishing fly.

137

'That's nice,' I said. 'Why?'

'Oh, Ma, really! It's Dunster Show!'

'Good Heavens!' I exclaimed. 'Has it come round already?'

'Surely you're going?'

Michael moistened his forefinger and manipulated the feather into position.

'Oh, I don't know, darling,' I said. 'I haven't been since I went with your father, the year before he died.'

'Well, I do think you ought to come this year. Go on, you'll enjoy it, it'll be fun. Anyway, we ought to have *some* sort of celebration.'

Michael had passed his Law Society Finals with flying colours, thank goodness, and a feeling of mild euphoria now hung over the household.

'I think I deserve a bit of a knees-up!'

'Well, I might,' I replied, 'if the weather forecast's OK. Do you remember that terrible year when it absolutely *poured* and all the cars sank in the mud and had to be dragged out with tractors? Old Jim Teal must have made a fortune!'

But the day of the Show dawned bright and dry, though there was quite a nippy wind.

'I'll put up a few sandwiches,' I said to Michael at breakfast. 'You know how awful it is trying to get anything to eat in the Refreshment Tent, dreadful queues! What would you like, cheese or ham?'

'Both, please.' Michael was deep in the local paper. 'Good Heavens! The drama society's going to do Adrian Palgrave's play *Sea-change*.'

'Good God!'

'Your friend Geraldine's producing it.' Michael found the relevant paragraph. 'She says here that it's to be "in the nature of a tribute to a distinguished local author".'

'It'll be absolutely *dire*!' I exclaimed. 'It's a very pretentious play, all about Caliban and Ariel left behind on the island after the end of *The Tempest*. A lot of confused stuff about Good and Evil and higher and lower selves.'

'Crumbs.'

'Plus,' I added with relish, 'lots of overtones and undercurrents about Freed Nations after Colonial Rule.'

'Sounds like a real dog's breakfast!'

'It is.' I said. 'They did it on the Third Programme, and even with a marvellous cast it was quite awful. What Geraldine will make of it, I can't imagine.'

'Well, you needn't see it,' Michael said reasonably.

'Don't you believe it,' I said, as I cut up bits of ham to fit the bread. 'My conscience will force me to go. I must just be careful *not* to go with Will Maxwell, else I shall certainly disgrace myself by laughing.'

'How is Will?' Michael asked. 'Have you seen him lately?'

'No.' I concentrated on fitting some little cakes carefully into a plastic box. 'He asked me to dinner last week, but I was busy.'

This was not strictly true. But ever since I had thought of Will as a possible murderer, I hadn't really felt able to face him. I was quite sure he couldn't have killed Enid in that horrible way. But, unlike Freddy Drummond, he had no other reason for wanting to burn down the Old Schoolhouse. Perhaps, I thought, the two deaths weren't connected at all. Perhaps someone (Will?) had murdered Adrian, and then someone *else* (Freddy Drummond?) had started the fire to destroy the papers. I was now thoroughly confused and uncertain and it seemed better to avoid everyone connected with the case for the time being. I should have realized, from past experience, that Dunster Show was not the best place to do this.

Chapter Fourteen

Even though we'd got there quite early, the showground was crowded. There were some holiday-makers, but mostly it was locals. They were either congregated around the livestock section, leaning knowledgeably over the pens, or in the huddle of horse-boxes, giving a final shine to the already sleek coats of horses, which either stood patiently, apparently bored by the whole business, or plunged about nervously, a hazard to be skirted with care.

Michael and I wandered around the pens for a while admiring the animals ('Who *does* that Exmoor shorthorn remind you of?') until he saw a friend and darted off ('See you back at the car for lunch'). I walked slowly round the stalls, looking at the pottery and woodcarving – such a lot of it, now that so many young people seemed to have set up little work-shops in a hand-to-mouth attempt to leave the rat-race in the cities.

'It all looks the same now, doesn't it?'

Rosemary, with Delia in a pushchair, paused beside me, looking at a trestle table set out with wooden table-mats, toast-racks, napkin rings, and a few overpriced pieces of furniture.

'I know,' I agreed. 'And the pottery, too, everywhere you go, from Windermere to Tintagel!'

'I'm just looking for the sheepskin place to see if they've got a pair of mittens that will fit Delia.'

I walked along beside them, Rosemary having some difficulty in easing the push-chair over the ruts in the grass and Delia hurling a blue woolly lamb to the ground to see how often we were prepared to pick it up for her.

'Jilly's with Jack watching the judging,' Rosemary said, 'but Delia got bored. She's too young, really, but Jilly wanted to come because we always do. Actually, it's not too bad because we're in the Enclosure and we can at least get a drink and something to eat in the Members' Tent. Where are you?'

'Oh, we're with the common herd,' I replied. 'Peter and I used to be Members, but that's one of the things I've sort of let slip since he died. Actually, I only came this year because Michael wanted to.'

'Well,' Rosemary said, looking around her at all the booths and stalls, 'it's certainly a bit different from when we used to come here as children.'

'Goodness, yes,' I replied. 'Then judging was the important bit and seeing your friends and the only display was a few tractors and the odd farm implement. Oh, and the Beer Tent! Now it's all police motor-cycle display teams and hamburger stands!'

'Well,' Rosemary said, 'it's still a place to see one's friends.' She gestured to where Oliver Stevens was standing, apparently lost in contemplation of a new disc harrow.

'He's looking very Lord of the Manor today,' I said, smiling. 'Look at those immensely hairy tweeds – he must be boiling! And where on earth do you think he got that marvellous fawn bowler hat?'

As we came towards him, Oliver turned and raised the bowler with a flourish.

'Ladies!' he said. 'How delightful to see you. Dunster Show is like Paris. If you stand still long enough everyone you know will eventually pass before you.'

'I mustn't stand still at all,' Rosemary said as Delia, bored with too much grown-up conversation, began to kick determinedly at the footplate of her push-chair. 'I'd better get Madam here back to the car before she becomes vocal. We hope she may become an opera singer

141

– certainly the power of her lungs would easily fill La Scala without any sort of amplification!'

'The trials of being a grandmother,' Oliver said, looking rather relieved that they had gone.

'Oh, she loves it,' I replied.

'It would have been pleasant to have had a child,' Oliver said, 'if it could have been born aged sixteen or so, with all the difficult years behind one.'

'There speaks the childless man.' I laughed. 'Up to sixteen is the easy bit!'

It was nice to feel comfortable with Oliver again, now that I knew he wasn't a murder suspect any more and that what I'd told Roger about our conversation on the train hadn't made trouble for him. Certainly Oliver himself seemed to have forgotten the whole incident. We chatted for a while until Sally suddenly materialized beside him.

'Oliver darling,' she said, slipping her arm through his with her usual proprietorial air, 'I've been looking for you everywhere. It's the middle-weight geldings next and I want you to see that chestnut of Harry Picton's.'

She was dressed in impeccable riding gear – the boots alone must have cost a small fortune – and looked even more relentlessly county than Oliver.

'Oh, hello, Sheila.' She belatedly acknowledged my presence.

'You're looking very professional, Sally,' I said. 'What are you showing today?'

'I've got quite a nice little mare and foal.' Sally, when talking about horses, was always a different person. 'And I have hopes of my new hunter. Class Thirty-two – but they're running late, of course.'

'Don't they always!' I said, as the tannoy suddenly leapt into life and demanded the presence of all weight-carrying cobs in the collecting ring.

They moved away and I decided that what I really wanted was somewhere to sit down. I was walking towards the bales of straw around the smaller of the two rings when I nearly collided with Will Maxwell.

142

'Sheila!' he said. 'Just the person! Come and have a drink before the lunchtime rush!'

I felt flustered and awkward. I hadn't really prepared myself to come face to face with Will. But within moments, as we picked our way through the thickening crowd, somehow we were back on our old footing. I simply *knew* (no sort of logic or reason) that Will couldn't have killed anyone, whatever the provocation, any more than I could myself. It was a tremendous relief – I hadn't admitted, even to myself, how important my friendship with Will really was. Still, now that I knew the extra dimension of tragedy surrounding Lucy's death, I felt even more strongly that I could never mention it to him, as I knew that he would never speak of it to me.

The refreshment tent was already quite crowded and I waited outside while Will fought his way in for the drinks. It was pleasant standing in the lee of the tent, out of the wind. The sun was really quite hot and the sound of the Taviscombe Silver Band playing its usual selection from *The Gondoliers*, together with the sweet smell of trampled grass, made me nostalgic for all the Show days of my youth. I stood there, mindlessly content, watching the people passing by when I was suddenly aware of a tall figure in black coming towards me. It was Father Freddy. My cheerful mood vanished and I looked around for some way of escape, but it was too late.

'Ah, Sheila, my dear. Such an agreeable occasion. A little crowded, perhaps,' he added, as a small girl, imperfectly in control of a determined-looking Exmoor pony, bore down upon us. We moved quickly out of the way and with a despairing cry of, 'Oh Gosh, I'm frightfully sorry . . .' she plunged on.

'Oh dear.' I laughed. 'Little girls and horses!'

The tannoy burst into life again.

'Will Major Amherst, who is judging Class Thirty-four, please come to the Committee Tent!'

'Are you here on your own?' Father Freddy asked.

'Michael's about somewhere,' I said, 'and Will Maxwell is in there getting me a drink. How about you?'

'Eleanor has very kindly invited me to have lunch with her in the Members' Tent. I was just making my way across to the Enclosure to meet her.'

'Oh, good. She's better, then? I thought she might not be well enough to come.'

'Better than she was, but not, I thought, really her old *self*, if I might put it like that.'

'That wretched flu thing does leave one feeling pretty down,' I said, 'and of course there's Robin . . .'

'She took it very hard,' he said gravely.

We stood for a moment in silence and I was relieved when Will appeared carefully carrying two drinks.

'I put the tonic in with the gin,' he said, 'because it was easier to carry, and there's lemon but no ice.'

He handed me a glass and smiled at Father Freddy.

'Hello. It's a really good turn-out this year, isn't it? Absolutely all one's chums. What can I get you, Father?'

'No, thank you, Will. I am on my way, as I was explaining to Sheila, to have lunch with Eleanor . . .'

'And there she is,' Will said waving. 'Eleanor! Over here!'

Eleanor didn't look quite as ill as she had done when I saw her last, but she still looked pale and drawn. For years she had never seemed to change, but today she looked her age. It wasn't just a physical ageing, lines and wrinkles and so forth, but the bounce and vitality had gone and the old schoolgirlish manner was subdued.

'Eleanor, my dear,' I said. 'How are you?'

She gave me a ghost of her former smile.

'I'm fine, right as rain, really.'

'I'm so glad to see you here,' I said.

'Couldn't miss a Dunster Show,' she replied. 'We've always come. Cousin Ernest used to be on the Committee.'

'How's Jessie?' I asked.

'Jessie?' Eleanor paused for a moment. 'Jessie's much better. She's here today somewhere. I think she said she wanted to see the WI produce stall.'

'Can I get you a drink?' Will asked.

'No thanks, Will, we'd better be getting along.'

As she and Freddy Drummond moved off together, Will looked after them and said, 'Two souls out of time.'

I was startled.

'What do you mean?' I said.

'Haven't you noticed? Those two – they don't really fit into this day and age, do they? I suppose that's why they get on so well together.'

'I agree about Father Freddy,' I replied. 'In fact, I was saying that very thing only the other day. And, yes, in a way, I do see what you mean about Eleanor. Not just the Angela Brazil schoolgirl bit, but there *is* something curiously old-fashioned about her. An attitude of mind, perhaps. She's always been a bit, well, unreal.'

'Being brought up by Cousin Ernest didn't help, I imagine,' Will said thoughtfully.

'No,' I replied. 'He was an odd sort of man. A very cold fish. I used to try and get out of going to tea with Phyllis and Eleanor when I was young in case he was there.'

'Was he disagreeable, then?'

'No, it wasn't that,' I said. 'I can't explain, really. He was very generous – tremendous going-home presents at parties and Phyllis and Eleanor had everything that money could buy in the way of toys and things. And then, when they were older, those very splendid tennis parties. He was always very *affable*, but there was no genuine warmth, there was always something under the surface. And – I've only just thought of this – he was always *there*. You know how it is when you're young, you don't want grown-ups around all the time. But he always seemed to be keeping an eye on us. It was a bit inhibiting!'

'What was Phyllis like?' Will asked.

'A very odd girl,' I replied. 'Difficult and nervy, their old nanny used to say. Withdrawn, almost. But of course not surprising, perhaps, with her mother dying quite young. She and Eleanor were very close when Eleanor was small, but when she was in her teens Phyllis withdrew even from her. She became quite obsessed about that boat of hers – went off on her own for days at a time. I expected Sir Ernest to object to that, but strangely enough he seemed to accept it. Then, of course, as you know, there was that accident.'

As I said the word I thought of Lucy and felt deeply embarrassed, but Will didn't seem to make the connection and simply said, 'Yes, it must have been awful for them – Eleanor and Sir Ernest.'

'Yes,' I said slowly, 'I'm sure they were very upset. But we didn't see much of them because they went abroad immediately afterwards, and when they came back they never mentioned it.'

'No,' Will said, 'I can see that they might not.'

'They did travel quite a bit,' I said hastily to change the subject, 'after Sir Ernest retired.'

'I came across them in Vienna once,' Will said, 'years ago, in the days when I was being a journalist. There was some sort of Foreign Office scandal – a young man, who'd been with Sir Ernest before he retired at one of his postings, in Italy, I think it was. He defected and my paper sent me out to get a comment.'

'Goodness,' I said. 'Do you think Sir Ernest was a spymaster!'

'I wouldn't think so; there was never any suspicion of that,' Will replied. 'But I remember thinking at the time how curiously unmoved he was about the whole affair. When I first approached him and said I was from the press he was very abrupt. He wouldn't speak to me. Foreign Office training, no doubt, but when I mentioned this man and the suspicions about him he changed completely and gave me a perfectly good interview. I suppose as long as he wasn't involved himself he didn't mind.'

'Oh, I'm sure Sir Ernest would have been very upset if anything threatened to dent his own perfect image,' I said cattily.

'There was something – I never quite pinned it down,' Will said. 'Something that wasn't quite right about him.'

146

'I would have liked to think that he was a spy,' I said, 'if only because that would rationalize my feeling of dislike for him!'

Will laughed, and taking my glass disappeared once more into the Refreshment Tent. When he emerged Michael joined us and we made our way over to the car for lunch. As I unpacked boxes of food and flasks from the boot I happened to look across the lines of cars and saw Jessie, leaning on the bonnet of an old Morris Minor. She was bent over and looked as if she might be ill. I thrust the sandwich box into Michael's hands and said, 'Can you carry on here? I'll be back in a minute.'

I hurried over to where Jessie was still standing.

'Jessie,' I called urgently out as I approached her, 'are you all right?'

She turned sharply at the sound of my voice and straightened up and I had the feeling that my attention was unwelcome to her. As she stood upright and faced me, with a curious mixture of embarrassment and defiance, I saw why. Jessie was unmistakably pregnant.

Chapter Fifteen

I simply didn't know what to say. I wasn't sure if I should comment on her condition or ignore it. I spoke tentatively.

'Jessie, what's the matter? You looked as if you might be ill.'

She acknowledged my obvious concern with a half-smile and said, 'I just felt a bit giddy for a minute, thank you, Mrs Malory, but I'm all right now.'

'Can I fetch Eleanor? Or would you like me to run you back to Kinsford in the car?'

'No. No, please don't disturb Miss Eleanor. I'm all right, really I am, thank you all the same.'

'Well, let me get you a cup of tea or something.'

'No, honestly, Mrs Malory, I'd rather you didn't bother. I don't need anything. I'll just go and have a bit of a sit down in Miss Eleanor's car. You get a bit tired, being on your feet for any time, when you're like this.'

This tacit admission of her condition emboldened me to say, 'When is the baby due?'

'I've got another three months to go.'

There was a silence, since Jessie seemed disinclined to say any more and there was no way that I could ask the one thing that I really wanted to know. After a moment I said, 'Well, if you're really sure there's nothing I can do . . . Take care of yourself.'

As I walked back to the car my mind was seething with queries. Michael and Will were half-way through the sandwiches when I rejoined them. Michael held out the tin.

'Here, have a ham one – there's only a couple left.'

As I took a sandwich automatically, Will looked at me curiously.

'What's the matter? You look upset.'

'I've had a bit of a shock,' I said. 'That was Jessie over there. She's pregnant.'

'What!'

Will and Michael stopped eating in astonishment.

'Not *Jessie*! Never!' Michael exclaimed.

'It's patently true,' I replied. 'She's six months pregnant.'

'But who's the father?' Will asked.

'I don't know. She didn't say and, obviously, I couldn't ask. Of course,' I added, 'that explains what she was doing at the doctor that time and why she's looked ill.'

'When did you see her last? Didn't you notice anything?'

'Not really,' I replied. 'When I met her at the doctor's she was wearing a mac, quite a full one, and when I called at Kinsford she had one of those old-fashioned wrap-around overalls on, very concealing.'

'I suppose,' Michael said thoughtfully, biting into the last of the sandwiches, 'she chose to come to Dunster Show to let everyone know. I mean, it's like taking a full-page advertisement in the *Western Daily News*!'

'Yes,' I said, 'though she was very embarrassed. So was I, for that matter! And Eleanor didn't say anything when I saw her earlier.'

I poured the coffee while Will and Michael went on expressing surprise at the news and speculating on the identity of the father, but I couldn't join in. I felt a wave of great sadness for Jessie. Behind her colourless remarks I had sensed a tremendous feeling of misery and something else that I couldn't quite define, almost despair.

'I suppose she's still only in her mid-thirties,' Will was saying, 'and in a way rather attractive – that dark hair

149

and high colouring. It's just that one never thought of her as having a boyfriend. Perhaps he'll marry her. Eleanor would miss her if she left.'

'Perhaps he can't marry her,' I said. 'Perhaps he's married already.'

'Well,' Will replied, 'I'm sure Eleanor would stand by her. Anyway, Jessie must want the baby or she'd have done something about it by now.'

'Yes,' I said doubtfully. 'But she didn't *seem* particularly happy about it. I know that in this day and age the single-parent family seems to be the norm rather than the exception, but Jessie is old-fashioned. I felt that she was ashamed of her condition. But, being old-fashioned, perhaps she wouldn't think of an abortion.'

'Poor Jessie,' Michael said. 'But never mind, look on the bright side. I bet Eleanor would love to have a baby about the place. It'll be spoilt rotten!'

This slightly more cheerful aspect of the affair did alleviate the depression that had descended upon us, and by the time we had each had a couple of swigs from Will's hip flask ('essential Dunster Show equipment') we were well on the way to considering Jessie's baby as something in the nature of a blessing.

The next day was a Saturday and I returned from my morning's shopping to find that Michael had covered the kitchen table and all the available work-top space with saucers and small bowls full of water, with what appeared to be pieces of paper floating about in them.

'Michael! Whatever are you doing!'

'Oh, hello Ma. The most extraordinary thing. I've found my old stamp collection.'

'Oh no!'

'I was tidying up my room, as you asked me to,' he said virtuously, 'and I was shoving some things onto the top shelf of my cupboard and the album fell out. And all these stamps I never got around to sticking in.'

He picked up one of the saucers and tilted it from side to side, spilling water on to the floor.

'These are all those African ones Uncle John sent me years ago from Zaïre and Mozambique – but of course I've got to float them off the bits of envelope first.'

I sighed.

'How long is it going to take? I mean, I can't really get lunch if there's nowhere to put anything down!'

'Oh, I won't be in to lunch, didn't I tell you? I'm seeing Mark in the Ship at twelve thirty.'

He looked at his watch and exclaimed: 'It's quarter-past now, I must dash.'

'But what about all this?' I asked. But he was gone.

I looked around the cluttered kitchen and decided that I too would have lunch out.

Since the season was still in full swing I knew better than to try any of the Taviscombe cafés, so I drove out to a small pub I know, off the beaten track and relatively free of summer visitors. It was a fine day and so I took my lunch (a rather good homemade pasty and a salad) to one of the tables outside, opened my book, and prepared to enjoy a peaceful half-hour. I was, therefore, irritated when I heard a voice at my elbow enquire, 'May I join you?'

My irritation turned to embarrassment when I saw that my companion was Freddy Drummond. True, I had seen him briefly at Dunster Show, the day before, but I was unprepared for what seemed likely to be a longish tête-à-tête.

'Of course,' I said, rather flustered, moving my book off the table and making room for him. 'How lovely to see you.'

He put down a plate piled high with cold meats and salad and another with what appeared to be the larger part of a French loaf and butter.

'The food here,' he said, 'is simple but plentiful. I usually come on the good Mrs Darby's day off.'

'Yes,' I said, 'I believe it's been featured in one of the good food guides, so it's sometimes quite crowded.'

He settled himself comfortably and began to work his

151

way through the mountain of food before him. I picked at my pasty, my appetite gone. After a few minutes he paused and regarded me quizzically.

'Poor Sheila,' he said, 'it must be embarrassing for you. I feel I owe you an apology.'

'What do you mean?' I asked.

'I have had a visit from your young friend in the CID,' he said.

'Oh dear.' I found myself saying apologetically, 'I'm sorry.'

'My dear child, it is not you who should apologize – it was an intolerable position in which to find yourself.'

'I had to tell Roger what was in the Meredith papers,' I said defensively.

'Of course. I am only distressed to think that you should have been upset at having to do so.'

He picked up a leaf of lettuce in his fingers and ate it meditatively.

'It was inevitable that Meredith should have kept copies of his correspondence,' he said. 'He had a considerable sense of his own importance and was quite sure that every last laundry list would be of intense interest to his devoted readers. As a biographer of some distinction yourself, my dear, you will appreciate the motives behind this vanity.'

'I know,' I replied, 'that Adrian was delighted at the amount of unpublished material there was.'

'Ah, Adrian,' he said. 'An excellent man of letters – to use a term now out of favour – but a thoroughly disagreeable human being.'

'Was he blackmailing you?' I asked bluntly.

'Blackmailing?' Freddy Drummond considered the word. 'No, I don't think one could call it that. He simply told me – and in a rather distasteful way – that he was going to use what he called "some rather compromising material" that concerned my younger days.'

'What did you say?' I asked.

'I quoted the great Duke, of course. "Publish and be damned." '

152

'I see,' I said doubtfully.

He regarded me benevolently.

'My dear child, do you imagine that this is the first time that such a situation has arisen? I have known many of the great and good – and, indeed, not so good – whose lives have been picked over by the literary vultures (present company excepted, of course). The more regrettable moments of my misspent youth (and I do, indeed, regret them) have been the subject for more than Meredith's correspondence.'

'But never published?' I asked.

He gave a little half-smile. 'I have a very good lawyer,' he said, 'and the libel laws of this country are, thank goodness, still quite effective. When I am dead, of course, there will be nothing I can do. As the wife of a lawyer you will doubtless remember that one cannot libel the dead. However, until that day, I have found that a strong warning has usually been sufficient.'

'I'm very glad,' I said.

'So you see, my dear, I had no motive – I believe that is the phrase used in such cases – for murdering Adrian. No *personal* motive, that is. As a priest and a Christian I must naturally believe that there is good in all men, but in the case of Adrian Palgrave I begin to wonder if the Almighty might have made an exception.'

He spoke these words gravely, quite unlike his usual flippant manner of speech, and I had the feeling that something more than personal distaste for the man lay behind it.

The young waitress came out to collect our plates.

'Would you like a sweet?' she asked me.

'No thanks, just coffee, please.'

Even if I had been hungry to begin with, the sight of Father Freddy demolishing that great plateful of food would have been enough to destroy my appetite.

The girl turned and smiled at my companion.

'The usual for you, Father?' she asked.

'Yes, please, my dear. And another drink for the lady.

Sheila, what shall it be? This' – he indicated his glass – 'is a very respectable Niersteiner, quite light and refreshing for a summer's day.'

'No, thank you,' I said. 'I'm driving. Oh well, perhaps an orange juice, then.'

'The manners and morals of each age,' Freddy Drummond said, 'influence and mould the thought and actions of the youth of that age. That is a truism, I know, but none the less accurate. When I was young there was a particular kind of hedonism, the result, they tell us, of the horrors of the First World War. I choose to think that it was just something in the air, the Spirit of the times, the *Zeitgeist*, that seemed to cast a spell on some of us. There is, goodness knows, an equal permissiveness today, but it is a relatively joyless thing, simply making a point, I sometimes feel, earnest and almost,' he laughed, '*political*.'

'Yes,' I said, 'that does come through, somehow, in the letters and memoirs of the twenties. There was a feeling of *something*. Goodness knows it wasn't innocence, since some of the behaviour was perfectly appalling.' I recollected to whom I was talking and stammered, 'Well, you know what I mean.'

'Indeed,' he said. 'And you are quite right to condemn it.'

'But it *was* different,' I said. 'I know that evil is evil, wherever and whenever it occurs, but . . .'

'I think that the word you are looking for is "style". Which, my dear Sheila, is simply self-deception, and it was, of course, our excuse for everything. The so-called Bohemian world of the twenties was quite small and, mercifully, had very little influence on the lives of ordinary human beings, so I always try to persuade myself that we were merely *self*-destructive. I thank God that I came to see His purpose, even if it was only at the end of my life.'

I looked at him curiously. This was a Freddy Drummond I had never seen before and I found I liked him better without the flourishings and the histrionic manner.

I felt I could tell this man how worried I was about Jessie.

'Is Jessie all right?' I asked tentatively. 'I had such a shock when I saw her at Dunster Show. I – we, none of us, had any idea . . .'

'Ah, yes, Jessie, the poor soul. She has spoken to me about her trouble.'

'Do you know who the father is?'

'Yes, yes I do.'

'Will he marry her?'

'No, that is not possible. Nor would she have wanted to marry him, if it had been.'

'Oh dear.'

We sat in silence for a moment and then he suddenly said, 'We must pray that the sins of the fathers will not be visited upon this small, new life.'

I was about to question him about this gnomic utterance when the girl reappeared with my orange juice and a plate laden with apple pie smothered with clotted cream.

Freddy Drummond smiled.

'Gluttony, the last, best sin,' he said, with a return to his old manner.

I leaned forward.

'I got the impression,' I said, 'that Jessie is deeply unhappy about this baby. Is that because it will be illegitimate or because of who the father is?'

'Both.'

I heard Dorothy Browning's voice in my head.

'Dark, a high complexion, rather gypsyish.'

'Adrian Palgrave was the father, wasn't he?' I asked.

Freddy Drummond scraped up the last of the apple pie and pushed his plate to one side.

'Do you have any reason for saying that?' he asked.

'It's just come back to me,' I replied. 'What somebody said about seeing them together once. It *is* true, though, isn't it?'

'Yes, it is true. I'm sure you will not make this generally known. It is not a pleasant situation for her.'

'No, I can see that. But Eleanor knows too, of course?'

'Indeed. She has been a great support to Jessie all through this dreadful business.'

'Did she know that Jessie and Adrian were having an affair?' I asked curiously.

'I think it was a great shock to her when Jessie told her about the baby,' he replied. 'Palgrave wanted her to get rid of it, of course.'

'I imagine he might have done. But Jessie wouldn't?' I asked.

'She is an old-fashioned woman and such a course was abhorrent to her. She knew that he would never leave his wife and marry her, but that was not what seems to have worried her.'

'Then what was it?' I persisted. 'I mean, if she wasn't worried about keeping the baby and if Eleanor was being kind and supportive, why is she obviously so unhappy about it all?'

He was silent for a moment and then he said, 'I honestly don't know. Like you, I have sensed something there that neither Jessie nor Eleanor will talk to me about. I don't know what it is, but it is eating away at them like a cancer. They are both deeply unhappy.'

'Of course,' I said, 'Eleanor is still very upset about poor Robin. And perhaps Jessie really did love Adrian and is grieving for him.'

But as I spoke I remembered Jessie's calmness and the matter-of-face way she had behaved on the evening that he had died.

'Oh God!' I exclaimed. '*She* found Adrian's body!'

'Yes,' he replied quietly, 'I have thought a great deal about that. I have, indeed, tried to talk to her about it, but she always turns the subject.'

'And Eleanor?' I asked.

'Eleanor confines herself to practicalities,' he replied. 'As is her way. Doctors and midwives and such. She will support Jessie and the baby financially, I believe. I imagine she wishes things to go on as before.'

I finished the last of my orange juice and said, 'I wish

there was something I could do. It's awful to see two good, kind people so unhappy and not be able to help in any way.'

Freddy Drummond looked at me steadily.

'There is another truism, and one that I, myself, cling to: that suffering purges the soul of sin and that through suffering we can come to the blessing of peace and love.'

As I got up to go he raised his hand, not in the gesture of mock benediction that he usually affected, but in a movement of genuine compassion.

Chapter Sixteen

I was in the pet shop getting some peanuts for the birds. I know you're not supposed to feed them in the summer, but *my* birds (finches, sparrows and robins as well as blue tits) have found that if they tap on the window often enough I am fool enough to go out and replenish their feeder, no matter *what* the season of the year. While I was in the shop I stocked up on this and that and eventually found that I had a great cardboard box, so full I could hardly lift it.

'Here, let me,' said a voice behind me and I turned to find Will.

'Oh, marvellous,' I said. 'I would be grateful. My car's miles away.'

'Just let me get some tins for Mac and I'll be with you.'

Mac, short for Macavity, is the inscrutable black cat who occasionally graces Will's cottage, when, that is, he isn't off hunting for rabbits on the moor, an arrangement that suits both of them perfectly.

We walked slowly up the hill to my car, chatting idly of nothing in particular, but when he had put the box in the boot Will said, 'Do you mind if I sit down for a few minutes? There's something I want to talk to you about.'

'Of course,' I said, as we both got into the car. 'What is it?'

'It's Jessie. I'm very worried about her.'

'I'm sure there's something very wrong there,' I agreed. 'I mean, more than just the obvious things. I saw Father Freddy the other day and he's worried, too.'

158

'I saw her last week,' Will said. 'Right out on the moor, over towards Weir Water. I can't imagine how she got there; she doesn't drive, does she? And it's miles from Kinsford. Anyway, I was out walking – trying out a new first act in my head – and I saw this figure sitting on a low stone wall. As I got nearer, I saw that it was Jessie. You can imagine my surprise! She looked dreadful. Not ill, but, well, what I can only call *haunted* – as if the Eumenides were after her.'

'Good Heavens!' I exclaimed. 'So what did she say?'

'That's the strange thing. Jessie and I have always got on rather well together, quite chatty and all that. But as I got closer and she could see who I was, she got up and quite deliberately turned away and went into a little wood. She so obviously didn't want to speak to me that I somehow couldn't follow her, although I was really very worried about her and how she was going to get home and everything.'

'What an extraordinary thing,' I said.

'I wondered if perhaps it was some sort of depression, something that expectant mothers get.'

'A sort of *pre*-natal depression? No, I'm sure there's something else, something very fundamentally wrong. Jessie has always been such a practical, *sensible* person. I would have thought she would be the *last* person to go all broody.'

'Do we know what Eleanor thinks about it all?'

'Father Freddy says she's being very supportive, financially and in every other way.'

'Won't the father contribute?' Will asked.

I hesitated and then said, 'I don't think he can.'

Will looked at me narrowly.

'You know who it is, don't you?'

I shifted in my seat and placed my hands on the steering wheel. 'I sort of put two and two together and Father Freddy confirmed my guess.'

There was a short silence and then Will said, 'Palgrave was the father, wasn't he?'

'Yes.'

'Do you think she's grieving for him, is that it?'

'No. No, I'm sure it's not. In fact, the extraordinary thing is that when she found his body she was so, well, composed is the only word for it. Quite calm, detached almost. The more I think about it – and I've been thinking about it a lot since I found out that he was the father, as you can imagine – the more unnatural it seems.'

'I suppose she might have been in a state of shock,' Will suggested.

'No,' I replied slowly,' it wasn't like that. The way she looked at the body' – I shuddered as I remembered what we had both seen – 'it was quite impersonal.'

'Do you think,' Will asked, 'that she knows who killed Adrian?'

'I think she must,' I replied. 'There's no other explanation for her behaviour.'

'Unless . . .'

'Unless,' I repeated, 'unless she killed him herself.'

We were both silent again.

'It really was the most Hardyesque scene,' Will said eventually. 'Out there on the moor. Pure *Tess*.'

'She killed her betrayer?'

Will shook his head. 'We mustn't get carried away,' he said. 'It would be ridiculous to let our judgment be influenced by literary fantasies.'

'Even so,' I said. 'Even if she didn't kill Adrian herself, I'm pretty sure she knows something about it.'

'What can we do?' he asked.

'I honestly don't know. The thing is, whatever Jessie may or may not have done, I can't help feeling desperately sorry for her.'

Early next morning something else happened that gave me cause for concern. The telephone rang while we were having breakfast.

'Michael, answer the phone, will you,' I said. 'If I leave this wretched toaster it'll fling the bread out on to the floor. Anyway, it's probably one of your little friends.'

I heard a little murmur of conversation and then Michael came back into the kitchen.

'It's your chum Roger,' he said. 'Classified information, by the sound of it. He wouldn't tell me, even though I told him that you were chained to the toaster.'

I picked up the telephone with some misgivings.

'Roger?'

'Ah, Sheila. I thought you'd like to know. Your guess *was* correct. There were traces of blood on one of the candlesticks from St Decumen's. The same blood type as Adrian Palgrave. Congratulations.'

'No fingerprints?'

'No. It had been pretty thoroughly cleaned and polished (they're trying to identify the kind of polish that was used), but it's quite an ornate thing and there was a certain amount of blood in the engraving and chasing round the base.'

I was silent for a moment, and then I said, 'The church is always open. Anyone could have taken it.'

'True.'

'And,' I continued, 'I gather you've had a word with Father Freddy. I jumped to the wrong conclusion there. He doesn't seem to have a motive after all.'

'Well, not the blackmail one, certainly,' Roger agreed.

'I can't think of any other,' I said. 'And somehow I can't see him taking a candlestick from his own altar . . .'

'You're probably right.'

'Oh dear, it's all so awful. Do you think that Robin . . . ? I mean, the fire *might* just have been vandals.'

'It would certainly be a neat solution, but somehow I don't feel it's the right one,' Roger said.

'No,' I replied sadly, 'I'm afraid you're right. So what do you think?'

'It's a bit of a dead end,' he replied. 'Two obvious suspects would be your friend Eleanor or her housekeeper. If you eliminate Freddy Drummond, then they were the nearest to the church and the most familiar with it. But they were together in the kitchen, surrounded with people at the crucial time.'

161

'Yes,' I said quickly, 'yes, they were.'

'So probably all I can do is leave it alone for a bit,' he said, 'and see if anything develops. There's always a moment in a murder case when you have to do that. It sort of clears your mind. Well, I'd better get on. I'll keep you posted – and thanks again for your inspiration about the candlestick. Forensic may come up with something useful on the polish.'

'How extraordinary,' I said, 'if the whole thing were to rest on a small domestic detail like a brand of metal polish! It's like something out of Sherlock Holmes.'

'Well, you couldn't actually build a whole case on it; the defence would have it in ribbons. But it might be a pointer, which way to look. I'll be in touch. Goodbye.'

'What's the matter, Ma?' Michael said as I went back into the kitchen.

'This beastly murder,' I said. 'Oh, Michael, *do* use the marmalade spoon, that knife is all crumby.'

'Don't change the subject. What particular aspect of this murder is making you look so uncheered?'

I told him about the candlestick.

'I should think,' he replied, 'you'd feel quite chuffed that your remarkable powers of deduction have been so successful.'

'But it's so appalling! Who on earth could have done such an unspeakable thing? I mean, it's sacrilege, on top of everything else.'

'I suppose when you're about to commit a murder, then a little thing like sacrilege is neither here nor there.'

'That's another thing,' I went on. 'It really does mean that it was premeditated. The murderer didn't just get carried away by emotion and snatch up the nearest thing to hand. No, it must have been planned. That's somehow even more horrible.'

Michael gathered up his plate and mug and put them into the sink with a crash.

'I've got to go. I'm going to the Magistrates' Court in Taunton with Edward today. Some joker up for stealing traffic cones, if you can believe it! Still, we can't all hobnob with the higher echelons of the Law like you. Shan't be late, Don't *worry* about all this. Leave it to Roger. Go shopping with Rosemary or something, and take your mind off it.'

But as I washed the dishes and, later, as I made the beds and did a little desultory dusting, my mind was still churning around. Certainly Eleanor or Jessie could perfectly easily have slipped into the church and taken the candlestick. They were near at hand and in and out of the church quite often, so that the presence of either one of them would not have been remarked upon. The fact that they were together didn't, as Roger implied, give each of them an alibi. He had no idea (and I had not told him) just how devoted they were to each other. There was no way that Eleanor would betray Jessie. Especially if she felt, as she obviously did, that Adrian had treated her abominably.

And I also knew that although there were a lot of people milling about just before the concert started, Jessie would have allowed no one, except Eleanor of course, into her kitchen. And it was possible to get from there to the old dairy without going into the main house.

Foss, sensing my mood, as he always does, followed me round the house wailing and weaving about my feet. I stooped and picked him up, holding him in front of me and staring into his unblinking blue eyes, as if there I might somehow find the answer to all my problems. He hung supine for a moment in my hands, then gave a loud cry of protest, so I swung him up on to my shoulder and walked over to the window. It was a grey, brooding sort of day and the low cloud increased my feeling of depression.

'It's no good,' I said. 'I've got to go and see Eleanor and Jessie.'

I put Foss gently on to the windowsill, picked up my handbag, and set off before my courage had time to evaporate.

163

Chapter Seventeen

When I got to Kinsford it was still dull and overcast, but now there was a chilly wind so that I shivered as I got out of the car and wished I had put a cardigan over my summer dress.

Jessie opened the door. She looked really unwell and her face was puffy, as if she had been crying. I asked for Eleanor and she said, 'Miss Eleanor's just gone over to the church to do the flowers for the graves.'

'If you don't think she'll be long, can I come in and wait for her?'

Jessie let me in rather reluctantly.

'Just a minute,' she said, moving the Hoover out of the drawing room doorway. She bent down to unplug it and swayed slightly. I moved quickly over towards her and took her arm.

'Come and sit down, Jessie,' I said. 'You really shouldn't be doing this. I thought Mrs Carter came in to do the housework.'

'She's got this flu thing and I can't let the house go to rack and ruin . . .'

I guided her towards one of the big sofas and made her sit down. She sat uncomfortably on the edge of the seat and protested, 'I'm all right, Mrs Malory, really I am. I just came over a bit giddy. It was nothing.'

I gathered my courage, took a deep breath and said, 'Jessie – I know about Adrian Palgrave.'

She gave a startled exclamation and turned to face me, her dark eyes seeming to grow enormous as the blood drained from her face. She clasped her hands together tightly and said, 'You know?'

'Yes, that he was the father of your baby.'

She put her hands up to her face and began to cry with great wracking sobs.

'Jessie.' I put my arm around her shoulder and the weeping became more violent.

After a while she appeared calmer, though she continued to cry, but quietly and with what seemed a deeper anguish.

'There is something else, isn't there?' I said.

She nodded without speaking and I went on.

'It's to do with the murder, isn't it?'

She nodded again.

'Do you want to tell me?' I asked gently. 'You have to tell someone. You can't go on like this. It's so bad for the baby.'

The mention of the baby brought on another fit of weeping, but gradually she gained some sort of control of herself and said, 'You're right, Mrs Malory, I've got to tell someone. It's just that . . .'

'It involves Miss Eleanor, too,' I said. 'I know.'

She looked at me hopelessly.

'I can't keep the baby,' she said. 'He'll have to be adopted.'

'Jessie, what do you mean?'

She was crying again.

'How can I keep him,' she burst out, 'when I helped to kill his father?'

'You helped . . .'

She made a great effort to pull herself together and tried to speak more coherently.

'I knew it was wrong, him being married, and really, I didn't want . . . but he was after me all the time. He'd come when he knew Miss Eleanor was out. He kept on and on, stupid stuff, poetry and such-like. But he was such a good-looking man,' her voice was wistful now, 'and I'd never had anyone after me, not like that – except – but that was a long time ago.'

She was silent for a moment and then continued.

'There was this holiday cottage, miles from anywhere. We used to go there. No one ever saw us. I used to worry about his wife, but he said they'd settled to go their own ways long since and, I suppose, I wanted to believe him, though I knew in my heart that it wasn't true.

'When I knew I'd fallen for the baby I had to tell Miss Eleanor. When I told her about Mr Adrian she was very upset and angry. Not angry with me, you understand, she was always very good to me. He said—' her voice broke. 'He said I had to get rid of it. I couldn't do that, Mrs Malory. Well, you're a mother, you'd know how I felt.'

'Yes,' I said. 'I know how you felt.'

'And Miss Eleanor, she felt the same, she was horrified. Then Mr Palgrave came to see her. Not about me, something to do with some old letters he was making into a book. I don't know what it was all about, but it was something terrible. When he'd gone, Miss Eleanor, she was like a wild thing, pacing up and down the morning room, and the look on her face! I can tell you, Mrs Malory, it frightened me. I didn't recognize her!'

I put my hand on hers. It was icy cold.

'She said he wasn't fit to live and things like that. I didn't realize, but she meant it. She told me to tell him to meet me in the old dairy at half-past six so that we could talk about the baby. Then she went—' She broke off and turned her head away.

'She killed him?'

'Yes.' It was almost a whisper.

'With the candlestick she took from the church?'

Jessie turned and looked at me, her eyes open wide.

'You know?'

'Yes,' I said. 'I know about the candlestick.'

'Then she came back,' Jessie went on, quickly now, as if she couldn't tell me fast enough what had happened. 'I took the candlestick – she'd put it in the pocket of her skirt – there was some blood, but it didn't show because of the colours.'

166

Black and red, I remembered, black and red.

'Then she went on into the concert as if nothing had happened. I was in a terrible state. Well, you can imagine. Then at the interval she came and told me that she thought she'd lost her bracelet in the old dairy – the safety clasp wasn't very secure – and would I go and look for her.'

'How *could* she!' I burst out. 'How could she make you go and look at Adrian, like *that*!'

'She couldn't go herself, she had to talk to all the people, else they'd wonder why. She knew I'd do it for her. She said if anyone saw me to say that I was going for those dinner plates. That's what I did, when I saw you, Mrs Malory.'

'Yes,' I said,' I remember.'

'I found the bracelet, it was there all right, and then I looked at him. And do you know, Mrs Malory, I didn't feel anything. It wasn't the Mr Adrian I knew, just a man lying there . . .' She paused again, as if to consider this. 'It was only later,' she went on, 'when the baby started to grow, that I realized what I'd done. And everything went wrong. Poor Mrs Palgrave.'

'Eleanor *couldn't* have . . .' I protested.

'She never knew that Mrs Palgrave was there, Mrs Malory,' Jessie said earnestly. 'She would never have done *that*. She just wanted to get rid of those papers. She was in a terrible way, when she knew. And then there was Mr Robin.'

Tears came into Jessie's eyes again.

'Oh, Mrs Malory, I thought she'd die when she heard about that. She went up to her room and wouldn't come out for two days. Nothing to eat. And I heard her crying, dreadful it was. She's never been like that since the day Sir Ernest was taken.'

'Poor Eleanor,' I said. 'Poor Jessie.'

'And what's to be done now, Mrs Malory?' she said. 'I don't know. She's so ill and moody. I'm afraid . . . I'm afraid it may have turned her mind.'

'The police know it was the candlestick that killed Adrian. They've found traces of his blood.'

'I gave it a good rub-up,' Jessie said, 'and put it back the very next morning.'

'So you see,' I continued, 'they'll put two and two together some time soon, even if I don't say anything.'

She caught my hand and said urgently: 'You won't say anything, Mrs Malory, not to the police!'

'Jessie, my dear, someone has got to. This can't go on. Leaving aside the question of right and wrong, look at what it's doing to you . . .'

'Please, no!'

She was hanging on to my arm, repeating the words over and over.

'All right, Jessie. I won't go to the police just yet. Eleanor must tell them herself. I'll go and find her.'

With a calmness I didn't feel, I got up and left the house. As I drove down to the church I tried to think coherently. I knew that Eleanor was obsessively protective of her cousin's reputation, but what could there have been about Sir Ernest in the Meredith papers that had frightened her so much that she was prepared to commit murder to prevent their publication? As Father Freddy had reminded me, the dead have no recourse to the law of libel. The letters must have been among those destroyed by the fire, for there'd been nothing about Sir Ernest in the ones I had read. I suddenly remembered what Will had said about the young man in the Foreign Office. So Sir Ernest had been some sort of spy. It all seemed fantastic and unreal, part of a television thriller, not real life.

The churchyard was empty; there was no sign of Eleanor. But, as I went in through the lych-gate, I saw that the door to the storage room where the mowers were kept was open and, approaching, I saw that there was a light on, so I went in.

Eleanor had just filled a watering can at the tap in the corner and had half-turned to see who had come in. I stood in the doorway and said, 'Hello, Eleanor.'

168

She straightened up and looked at me. Something in my face must have told her what I knew.

'Hello, Sheila.'

We stood facing each other for a moment and then she said, 'You know, don't you?'

'Yes,' I said sadly. 'I know.'

'But,' she said harshly, 'you don't know *why*!'

'Jessie,' I said, 'and Sir Ernest.'

She gave me such a fierce look that I instinctively stepped back a pace.

'What do you know about Cousin Ernest?' she demanded.

'That there had been some scandal in France years ago and that there were letters in the Meredith papers about it that Adrian was going to publish.'

'He *came* to me,' Eleanor said, 'and calmly told me that he was going to put them in this book, destroying the reputation of a man whose name he wasn't even fit to mention!'

'Would it have been so very bad?' I asked. 'It would have been a nine-days wonder. There are so many spy stories nowadays.'

'Spies? I don't know what you're talking about!' Eleanor said brusquely. 'It was nothing to do with spies. It was about Cousin Ernest and that child. Her parents made such a fuss, there was a scandal and he had to transfer.'

'A child!' I asked.

She suddenly burst out, 'All he wanted was love. Is that so much to ask? Even Phyllis, even his own *daughter* didn't understand. *I* understood, though. I loved him. I was the only one who understood.'

A sickening realization came over me.

'You mean – Phyllis?'

'The stupid girl,' Eleanor said scornfully. 'Leaving that note, saying she couldn't bear it any longer.'

'She killed herself? It wasn't a boating accident?'

'She said she felt defiled,' Eleanor spat out the word, 'and that there wasn't enough water in the world to make

169

her clean again. I destroyed the note before he saw it. He would have been so hurt. He was upset, of course, but she'd been difficult for ages and he had me – and then Jessie came, too.'

'Oh God,' I said, thinking of the two women shut up in that great house with that monstrous secret for all those years.

'It was *love*,' Eleanor repeated, staring at me fixedly. 'You do understand, don't you?'

I couldn't speak and stared back at her.

'I *had* to kill Adrian, you do see? There was Jessie as well. He betrayed her, wanted her to kill her baby. He tried to take a life.'

She shook her head as if to clear it.

'I had to destroy those papers. I *did* destroy them, didn't I? They say you've got them now.'

'Yes,' I whispered, 'you destroyed them.'

She gave a great sigh.

'I swear I didn't know Enid was there. Oh God, how I've thought and thought about that! And Robin! My poor Robin! But you do see that I had to do it? I *couldn't* let Adrian publish those awful things about him for people to read and snigger at and not understand. And Jessie . . .'

'What have you done to Jessie?' I said. 'How *could* you involve her like that!'

Eleanor looked at me sharply, as if actually realising for the first time who she was speaking to.

'You won't tell anyone about the papers, about Cousin Ernest?'

'I can't promise you that,' I said.

Eleanor gave me such a look of hatred and malevolence that I instinctively recoiled. I remembered Jessie's words about her being unrecognisable.

She came slowly towards me and I found that I was unable to move. I drew in my breath sharply and the cold, damp, charnel-house smell of the place caught me by the throat so that I thought I would choke.

A breeze from the half-open door caught the naked bulb, high in the ceiling, making the shadows move and casting its harsh light on Eleanor's distorted face.

She came right up to me until her face almost touched mine and I was rigid with fear. Instinctively I shut my eyes and prepared myself for the blow I knew must come.

Suddenly she gave a loud cry, harsh and torn with pain like a wounded animal, and pushed me with all her strength. I fell sideways and she rushed past, through the heavy oak door. For a moment I lay there. My head was hurting from where I had hit it against the wall and blood was oozing from my arm where it had been grazed against the cold, rough stone. The effort required to move seemed intolerable, but slowly I managed to get to my feet and stood in the doorway, supporting myself painfully against the massive doorpost. A fine driving rain was falling as I looked out across the churchyard.

Eleanor was lying on the grass beside Sir Ernest's grave, curled up like a child, sobbing as if her heart would break.